THE SECRET LIFE OF BETHANY BARRETT

By Claudia Mills

Macmillan Publishing Company
New York

Maxwell Macmillan Canada
Toronto
Maxwell Macmillan International
New York Oxford Singapore Sydney

Copyright © 1994 by Claudia Mills

Macmillan Publishing Company is part of the Maxwell Communication
Group of Companies.

Macmillan Publishing Company
866 Third Avenue
New York, NY 10022

Maxwell Macmillan Canada, Inc.
1200 Eglinton Avenue East
Suite 200
Don Mills, Ontario M3C 3N1

First edition
Printed in the United States of America
10 9 8 7 6 5 4 3 2 1
The text of this book is set in 13 point Caledonia.

Library of Congress Cataloging-in-Publication Data
Mills, Claudia.
The secret life of Bethany Barrett / Claudia Mills. — 1st ed.
p.   cm.
Summary: Eleven-year-old Bethany has a list of worries,
including her younger brother's speech development, the lack of
popularity of some of her friends at school, and especially the fear that
her mother can't cope with all of Bethany's worries.
ISBN 0-02-767013-9
[1. Worry—Fiction.   2. Mothers and daughters—Fiction.
3. Brothers and sisters—Fiction.   4. Schools—Fiction.
5. Friendship—Fiction.]   I. Title.
PZ7.M63963S1   1994
[Fic]—dc20   94-16663

To my Boulder writing friends:

Marie Desjardin
Claire Martin
Ann Nagda
Leslie O'Kane
Phyllis Perry
Ina Robbins
Elizabeth Wrenn

THE SECRET LIFE OF
BETHANY BARRETT

1
...

Bethany noticed the mistake with the balloons right away. As she blew up the first one, instead of swelling to say HAPPY BIRTHDAY, the small, shrunken letters on the side read GOOD LUCK. The second balloon said GOOD LUCK, too. And the third. Of course, GOOD LUCK was better for a birthday balloon than MERRY CHRISTMAS or GET WELL SOON. But Bethany knew that her mother had meant to buy balloons that said HAPPY BIRTHDAY, and now, with three blown up and twenty-two more to go, Bethany didn't know what to do.

She blew up a fourth balloon, yellow as a crayon

sun, and tied a knot at the end. Brandon's party was only an hour away. There was no time to bicycle back to the store for the right balloons. Her older sister, Brooke, might be able to drive to the store for some, but Brooke was on the phone. These days Brooke talked on the phone by the hour to a boy named David.

Maybe the best thing to do was pretend she hadn't noticed. Then, if her mother said anything, Bethany could say, "You mean, you didn't *want* the balloons to say 'good luck'?" She could act as if all the birthday parties she had ever attended in all her eleven years had had GOOD LUCK balloons everywhere.

Or she could just tell her mother, "Mom, the balloons are wrong." But it was so important to her mother that every detail about Brandon's party be perfect. Bethany couldn't break the news to her about a problem now, when it was too late to do anything to fix it.

But it's no big deal! Bethany wanted to shout. They're just dumb balloons. Brandon's only three. He can't read. He can barely even *talk*. But *balloon* was one of the 153 words Brandon could say. Bethany knew there were 153 words because her mother wrote all of Brandon's words in a special notebook that she kept in the kitchen drawer.

Bethany blew up another balloon, an orange one. Then she went into the kitchen to check on her mother's progress with the cake. It was a freight-train cake, made from a sheet cake cut into four pieces: one locomotive, one boxcar, one hopper car, and a caboose. Brandon loved trains. *Train* had been number eighteen on the word list.

"It's wonderful," Bethany said, and it was. Each of the four cars of the train was frosted in a different color, with all kinds of details added in thin lines of black icing.

"Do you think they'd hire me in the bakery department at King Soopers?" her mother asked, wiping a dab of red (caboose) frosting from her chin with the back of her hand.

"Tomorrow," Bethany said. "You'd be head baker supreme."

"Are you done with the balloons?" her mother asked.

"Almost." Bethany scooped a fingerful of frosting from the bowl. "It's kind of a lot of work blowing them up, though. Do you think we really need balloons?"

"Of course we need balloons!" her mother cried gaily. "A three-year-old's birthday party is all about balloons. Balloons, and cake, and pin the tail on the donkey. Can you run outside and tie a couple to the mailbox? So everyone will know that this is the house with the birthday party. Brandon's going to be back any minute from his ride with Daddy."

"Okay," Bethany said. Back in the living room, she blew up five more balloons and tied a length of string to each one. Everyone was going to know that this was the house with the good-luck party. But the mistake with the balloons didn't seem as serious as it had five minutes ago. It was just that her mother seemed so fragile sometimes. Like the china shepherdess Ma set on Pa's carved shelf in the Little House books.

Brooke came downstairs as Bethany finished blowing up the last of the balloons.

"Good luck?" she asked.

"I think Mom bought the wrong ones," Bethany said, suddenly feeling worried again. "But these'll be okay, right?"

"I'm all for good luck," Brooke said. "Leave them on the mailbox, and maybe I'll get six acceptances on April fifteenth."

4

Brooke was a high school senior. She had applied to six colleges, and Bethany knew that she would be accepted to all of them. Brooke was perfect. Bethany didn't resent Brooke for being perfect. Brooke couldn't help it; it was just the way she was.

Bethany looked out the window. "Brandon's here. Let's go watch what he does when he sees the cake."

A minute later Brandon raced into the house. At home he hardly ever *walked*: he ran, he danced, he pranced, he swaggered, he strutted, he bounced. It was as if the whole world were one big version of the trampoline that he was going to get for his main birthday present.

When he saw the cake laid out on the dining-room table, he stopped. "Brandon's cake?" he asked. "See it! See the train!"

"That's right," his mother said. "It's a cake train for you. For your birthday. When your friends get here, we'll put on three candles, and then we'll sing 'Happy Birthday,' and then we'll eat it."

"Brandon eat train!"

"And you'll get your presents, and we'll play games," Daddy said.

"I hope they can do pin the tail on the donkey," Bethany's mother said doubtfully. "I tried it with Brandon yesterday, and he didn't really understand that he was supposed to stick the tail on the donkey's rear end."

"They'll have fun, anyway," Brooke said. "I mean, the whole idea is just for them to have fun and not kill each other or destroy anything, right? Pin the tail is better than smearing red frosting on the walls."

"Or coloring on them," her mother said. "Bethany, honey, do you remember when that awful girl from your first-grade class came over to play and ended up coloring on the wallpaper in your room? What was her name?"

"I don't remember," Bethany said. She felt her cheeks flaming.

"Jane. Jane Owen. That's it. She would have had you coloring, too, I think, if I hadn't found some quick excuse to send her home. You wouldn't think one child could be a bad influence on another in the first grade, but that Jane had *troublemaker* written all over her."

"What ever happened to Jane?" Brooke asked. "Is she still in your school?"

6

"I don't know," Bethany said.

This was the fiftieth time her mother had told the coloring-on-the-wall story. In this family, if you made one mistake, you heard about it for the rest of your life. The time Daddy had filed the income tax late. The time Brooke had been so excited about the first day of school that she'd walked to school all by herself a day early and then cried because her teacher hadn't been there to greet her. The time Bethany and that awful Jane Owen had colored on the new wallpaper. What a *bad influence* Jane had been, and wasn't it a good thing that Bethany's mother had nipped *that* friendship in the bud.

"You bought the wrong balloons for Brandon's party," Bethany blurted out then. "They don't say 'happy birthday,' they say 'good luck.' "

She wanted to take the words back as soon as they were spoken. But it was better than saying what she had wanted to say for the past five years: coloring on the wall that time was my idea, not Jane's. I was the bad influence, not her.

"Oh, no," Bethany's mother said. Her eyes filled with tears, and Bethany was afraid she was going to cry. "Scott, do they look too silly? It's all my

7

fault. I grabbed the package off the shelf so quickly. . . . I hardly even looked—"

"They're fine, Anne," Bethany's father said soothingly. "No one's going to notice. You need good luck at a preschooler's birthday party."

"Party!" Brandon said. "See my party!"

Bethany's mother took one last despairing look at the balloons and then went to write down *party* in Brandon's word book.

Bethany's mother had told her that all the magazine articles on birthday parties said to invite the same number of children as the birthday child's age. So three children from the neighborhood were coming to Brandon's party: Tavi, Rosa, and Rosa's older brother, Ian.

Rosa and Ian arrived first. Ian was wearing jeans and an old green T-shirt, but Rosa had on a party dress of pink flowered material, smocked in front, with a huge pink bow in her curly hair.

"Is Brandon three, Ms. Barrett?" she asked. "I'm three, too. Ian's five. I was three in February. I got this dress for my birthday. My grandmother sent it to me from New York. She lives in New York. New York is far, far away. I'm going to visit her all by myself when I'm six, and she's going to take me to the Entire State Building."

"That's nice, honey," Bethany's mother said, but her voice sounded unsteady. Bethany knew it was always a shock to her mother to hear how much other three-year-olds talked.

"I'm going to be six first," Ian said. "When you're six you can be on the soccer team. I can already kick a soccer ball two miles."

"No, you can't," Rosa said.

"Yes, I can. One boy in my class at school can kick a soccer ball three miles, and I can kick it almost as far as he can."

Because Ian was five and so grown-up, Ian and Rosa's parents dropped them off and left right away. But Tavi's mother stayed.

Bethany didn't like Ms. Gordon. You could tell that she thought Tavi was the most brilliant and wonderful child in the world, and that no other child in the history of the planet could possibly compare.

"Happy birthday, Brandon!" Ms. Gordon said. "Are you all ready for your party?"

Brandon didn't reply.

"Are you all ready for your party?" his own mother repeated.

"Yes," Brandon said. Which was probably true, but Bethany knew that Brandon said yes to all questions, if he answered them. Maybe he didn't understand what he had been asked. Or maybe he was just trying his best to be agreeable and give the grown-ups the answer they seemed to want.

Tavi held out his present. "Here," he said. "It's a stuffed Barry Bear. I hope you like Barry Bear. It's my favorite show. I can sing all the songs on it. I can sing every single song."

"Tavi!" Ms. Gordon said, laughing. "You're not supposed to tell Brandon what's in his present. It's supposed to be a surprise."

"It's a *surprise* Barry Bear," Tavi said. "And I didn't tell what color it is. I didn't tell that it's purple."

"Oh, Tavi!" Ms. Gordon said, looking around to make sure that everyone else was marveling at Tavi's cuteness and funniness. "Really, I should write down the things he says and send them off to one of those parenting magazines."

Brandon took the present and looked uncertainly at his mother.

"We'll open it later," she said. "First, let's have some games. How about pin the tail on the donkey?"

"I *love* pin the tail," Rosa said. "I won first prize at Sara's party."

"I win first prize at every party," Ian said.

"So do I," Rosa said.

"You do not."

"Yes, I do."

"What's the prize?" Tavi asked. "What do you get if you win?"

"It's a surprise," Bethany's father said.

"Is it a purple Barry Bear?" Tavi asked.

"Tavi!" Ms. Gordon said. "Did you hear that? Now he thinks every surprise is a Barry Bear!"

Bethany watched her father blindfold each child in turn and hand him or her the donkey tail. Ian won easily, even though Bethany's father made him walk farther across the room for his turn. Rosa and Tavi each came close. But when it was Brandon's turn, he just stood still, clutching his cardboard tail, unsure what to do, until Brooke gently guided him forward.

Bethany couldn't stand it anymore. Even though Brandon was her own brother, and she loved him more than anything in the world, and this was his one and only three-year-old birthday party, she couldn't bear another minute of his not talking, not understanding, not *getting* it. Even more, she couldn't stand another minute of her mother's watching him with anxious eyes.

While Brooke was giving Ian his prize—a Barry Bear coloring book—Bethany slipped upstairs to her room and closed her door and lay facedown on her bed with a pillow over her head. She must have stayed there for at least half an hour, for when she made herself go downstairs again, the others were already singing "Happy Birthday." Brandon blew out his candles on the second try—Bethany's heart unclenched a bit—and he seemed delighted with his Barry Bear and a little wooden train from Ian and Rosa.

When his parents brought out the small, round trampoline, though, he froze with shyness and refused to try it.

"You go first, Brandon," Mr. Barrett said. "You're the birthday boy."

But Brandon just watched, wide-eyed, as Rosa, Ian, and Tavi each took turns jumping higher and higher.

"Don't you want to jump, honey?" his mother said.

Brandon shook his head.

Jump! Bethany tried to will him to step forward and try it, but he stayed at the edge of the carpet, his birthday hat sliding down the side of his head.

At last the party was over. Brooke walked Rosa and Ian back home, and Tavi's mother finally left with Tavi.

"Brandon's turn?" Brandon asked. "Brandon jump?"

His mother smiled. Bethany thought her smile looked shaky. Brandon ran over to the trampoline and jumped and jumped, his face aglow with pride.

"You can take the balloons down from the mailbox," her mother told Bethany. Bethany hurried outside, glad for another escape.

Somehow she had to make Brandon talk better, have real conversations with people the way the other children did. If only she could do it by tomorrow. Her parents would be so pleased and astonished, and she could parade Brandon in front of Tavi's mother and say, "See! Brandon talks better than Tavi now." Not that it was a contest. It wasn't. But still.

She wanted to *do* something. Maybe if she were brilliant and famous herself, it wouldn't matter that

Brandon didn't talk. Could you make yourself into a genius? If there was any genius in the family, it was Brooke, with her straight A's and sky-high SAT scores. But Bethany could try to be a second Barrett-family genius. She could get books out of the library on nuclear physics for sixth graders. Or, even better, she could start her own word list, a genius word list. She could look up lots of really hard vocabulary words to memorize, and figure out how to use them all in complete sentences. She'd start her own word book and write a new superhard word in it every day.

Bethany untied the cluster of GOOD LUCK balloons from the mailbox. She remembered that she had a small pair of scissors in her pocket for cutting the string. Then, suddenly, with a savagery that surprised her, she stabbed them, all five, each one in turn. Five GOOD LUCK balloons, five sharp holes, five small explosions.

2
...

Later that afternoon, Bethany loaded her back-pack with her dictionary and a small spiral-bound notebook and a piece of Brandon's train cake wrapped in a birthday napkin. "I'm going to the park!" she called to her mother. Then she walked three blocks down and three blocks over to Jane Owen's house.

Jane was usually in her tree fort, so Bethany didn't stop to knock at Jane's front door. She hurried into the Owens' deep backyard and gave the secret call up into the budding branches of Jane's tree: "B and J, J and B. Friends forever, you and me!"

In answer, a sturdy rope ladder came swinging down from the front entrance of the fort. Bethany climbed up without looking down. It was a long way up to the tree fort, and she didn't particularly like heights. But once she was up, it was wonderful to be safe and snug within the fort's four log walls.

Jane pulled the ladder back up again. Now no one could come after them.

"How was Brandon's party?" Jane asked.

"Fine," Bethany said. "Actually, it was horrible, but I brought you a piece of cake."

Jane rummaged in her treasure box and pulled out two plastic forks.

"I'm not hungry," Bethany said.

"I am," Jane said. "I'm always hungry."

It was true. Skinny Jane, all knees and elbows and bony angles, ate more than any other person Bethany had ever seen. In a moment the thick piece of green boxcar was gone.

"Horrible, how?" Jane asked then, as she licked the tines of the fork clean.

"Just horrible. My mother bought the wrong balloons, and I didn't want to tell her, but then I did, and the other kids all talked and talked like windup dolls, and Brandon wouldn't jump on his trampoline until they were gone, and it was bad enough when he was two and didn't really talk, but now he's three and doesn't really talk. And my mom told everybody again about how we colored on the wall that time."

"I'm part of the Barrett family history," Jane said. "Maybe if she tells about me often enough, I'll turn into a myth and legend, and children will learn about me in the myth-and-legend unit in third-grade language arts."

Bethany laughed. "She has it all backward, too. It wasn't your idea to color on the wallpaper; it was mine."

Jane thought for a minute. "It was both, really. You were the one who said you had new zoo wallpaper in your room, with lions and tigers and seals but no bears, and you wished you could draw some bears on it. And I was the one who said, 'Let's do it.' "

That sounded right. Bethany was usually the one who had the ideas, and Jane was the one who made them happen.

"Anyway," Bethany said, "I've decided that I need to become a genius."

Jane's eyes widened. "A genius? Like Einstein?"

"Well, more like Brooke. Just an ordinary genius. I think my mother would feel better if two of us were supersmart, given that Brandon—well, I don't know that he *isn't* a genius, but I don't think he is."

"He might be. Charles Wallace in *A Wrinkle in Time* didn't talk until he was almost four, and *he* was a genius."

"Does it sound really stupid, to try to be a genius?"

"No," Jane said. "I'll be a genius, too. It can't hurt. We'll both be geniuses. What do we have to do to get started?"

Bethany pulled her dictionary out of her backpack. "I thought we could learn one new really hard word every day. We can write them down in this notebook, and practice using them when we talk."

Jane pounced on the dictionary. "We can start with *A*. We can start with the first page of *A*'s and learn the hardest word on every page. I already know one hard word that starts with *A*: *antagonistic*. I got it on a report card once."

"What did it mean?"

"I think it meant that I talked back. To Ms.

Williams last year. Remember how I told her I wouldn't be in the Columbus play because Columbus killed too many Indians? She said I was antagonistic."

"How do you spell it?" Bethany asked.

"I'll look it up," Jane said. She thumbed through the pages. "Here it is. 'Antagonistic. Acting in opposition; hostile; counteracting.' I guess I was all of those things."

Bethany wrote *antagonistic* on the first line of the first page in the notebook. "Let's do another hard word today, one neither of us knows."

She looked over Jane's shoulder at the first page of *A*'s. "We're never going to use *abalone*," she said. " 'A large gastropod mollusk.' "

"*Aardvark* sounds pretty good," Jane suggested. "It says here, 'earth pig.' And there's even a picture."

"I already know *aardvark*," Bethany said. "They have aardvarks all the time on *Sesame Street*."

"What about *aardwolf*?" Jane pointed to the next entry. "I bet they don't have aardwolves on *Sesame Street*. 'Aardwolf. A quadruped mammal resembling a hyena in appearance and behavior and feeding mostly on carrion and insects.' "

"It sounds pretty horrible," Bethany said. "Do you think we'd ever use it in a sentence?"

"Donya Cabot is an aardwolf," Jane said. "Or you could use it as an insult:you aardwolf, you! Or: take that, you aardwolf!"

"That sounds pretty antagonistic to me," Bethany said. She didn't know why Jane didn't like Donya. Donya was too wrapped up in being popular, but other than that she was all right, really. Bethany's mother loved Donya. She thought Donya was Bethany's best friend.

"I'm only antagonistic to aardwolves," Jane said. "And we have a duty to act in opposition to aardwolves."

Bethany wrote *aardwolf* on the next line in the notebook. She and Jane were beginning to sound like geniuses already.

That evening, after Brandon had gone to bed, the phone rang at Bethany's house.

"It's for you," Bethany's mother said, holding out the receiver with a big smile. "It's Donya!"

"I'll take it upstairs," Bethany said. She didn't want her parents hearing how little she had to say to her supposedly best friend.

"Hi," she said, once she was lying on Brooke's daybed, with Brooke's pale pink phone to her ear. She heard the click of her mother hanging up the other extension. "How are you?"

"Fine," Donya said. "Did you do the math problems for Monday yet? They're really hard."

"No," Bethany said. "Not yet." Actually, she had done them the night before, and they hadn't been hard at all, but she didn't like it when Donya teased her about being good at math. Nobody teased Brooke about getting A's.

"I hate math," Donya said. "It's like, why did they invent calculators if we still have to change fractions to decimals and decimals to fractions? It's like, there's no point to it. Anyway, forget math. I'm having a party. Two weeks from today, and you're invited. Everybody is, except Nicole. And the boys. Or should I invite the boys? Evie says I should."

Evie was supposedly Bethany's second-best friend. But Bethany liked Nicole a lot more than she liked Evie, even though the popular girls picked on Nicole because she was fat and her T-shirts were too tight. During the library reading program last summer, Nicole had read the most books of anybody in their grade. Bethany loved to read, too. A book report Nicole had done in class a couple of years ago had started Bethany reading the Little House books, and they had become her all-time favorites.

"I wouldn't invite boys," Bethany said. "But don't you think—I mean, Nicole is going to feel awful when she finds out."

"My mother said I could have twelve girls," Donya said, "and Nicole would make thirteen. I can't help what my mother says."

"But if you invite the boys that would make more than twelve."

"She said twelve *girls*. Obviously, if I invited the boys, it would have to be more than twelve. Did anyone ever tell you you're a worrywart? I mean, there's always somebody who doesn't get invited to things. So about the boys: I can't decide. Should I invite them or not?"

"I don't know. Listen, I have to go. Brooke needs the phone."

Bethany put down the receiver harder than she meant to. She didn't want to go to Donya's party if Donya was going to be such an—aardwolf—about inviting Nicole. But Donya's mother was in a women's club with her mother, and if she didn't go, Donya's mother might say something to her mother about it at their next meeting. Maybe Bethany could just explain—but she wasn't very good at explaining things to her mother. Whenever anything in Bethany's life wasn't absolutely wonderful, her mother's eyes looked so large and sad, and the little wrinkle lines in her forehead grew even deeper.

Just because you worried about things didn't make you a worrywart. Some people just happened to have a lot of things to worry *about*.

On the other hand, Bethany knew that she worried more than most people. She even had a special chart for keeping track of her worries, which she kept under the blotter on her desk. On the top of the page she'd written PROBLEMS. For each problem on the chart, Bethany wrote down how serious it was (Not Serious, Pretty Serious, Very Serious, Very Very Serious), what she could do about it, what she was learning from it, and what good thing she had in life to make up for it. Since she had started the list, back in September, Bethany had never shown it to anyone, not even Jane.

Bethany put Brooke's phone back on her night

table and went to her own room to add Donya's party to the problems list.

Problem: Donya's party
Seriousness: PS
What to do: Just go, but be extra nice to Nicole at school?
What learned: Beware of aardwolves!
Good thing: Jane

Then Bethany looked over the rest of the items currently on the list.

Problem: Social studies report on Afghanistan
All the good books from the library are checked out
Seriousness: PS
What to do: Try to find magazine articles *National Geographic*?
What learned: Next time, start sooner
Good thing: A's in English, math, science

Problem: Torn zipper on jeans
Seriousness: NS

What to do: Tell Mom when she is not too frazzled
Wear something else in meantime
What learned: Nothing
Good thing: Pizza for supper on Tuesday

Problem: Brandon's talking
Seriousness: VVS
What to do: ???
What learned: ???
Good thing: Everything else about Brandon

Bethany erased the question marks beside "What to do" and penciled in: "Make it up to Mom by becoming a genius."

After lunch on Sunday, Bethany got ready to go to Jane's house again.

"Where are you going, honey?" her mother asked.

"Just for a walk," Bethany said.

"Would you take Brandon with you?"

"Sure," Bethany said. She knew Brandon wouldn't tell where they had been. There were certain advantages to having a brother who didn't answer questions.

Of course Brandon couldn't climb a rope ladder, either. Jane came down from the fort and led Brandon and Bethany into the kitchen for cookies and milk. Jane's mother, as thin and bony as Jane, gave them each a welcoming hug and disappeared to her study upstairs.

"Slice and bake," Jane said. She held out a packaged tube of chocolate-chip cookie dough. "We can bake them or just eat the dough."

"Dough," Bethany said.

The girls put Brandon in charge of slicing it with a dull plastic knife.

"Watch me!" he said. "Brandon do it. Brandon chop."

It took Brandon a long time to slice the dough, so Bethany and Jane opened the dictionary to the second page of A's.

"Here's one," Bethany said. "*Abdominous*. 'Big-bellied.'"

"Nicole McCloskey is abdominous," Jane said. "But it's not her fault. Her parents are fat, too. Some people just are. Did you know that Donya is having a party, and she's inviting all the girls in our class except Nicole?"

"She told me," Bethany said. "She called last night."

Bethany concentrated on the long list of entries on the next page in the dictionary. "Here," she said. "I found another one. Listen to this. *Abhor*. 'To shrink from in fear, disgust, or hatred; detest to extremity.' "

Jane looked where she pointed. "It's wonderful! Is there anyone we abhor? I don't abhor Donya. You can't really abhor aardwolves. You pity them."

"The new librarian at school, Mr. Zucaro? I think I might abhor him," Bethany said. "It's like he hates books and hates to have anybody touch them. You know how he yells at people all the time in that really mean, sarcastic way."

"Do you shrink from him in fear, disgust, or hatred?" Jane asked.

"No," Bethany had to admit. "I don't detest him to extremity, either. I detest him a lot, though. I *almost* abhor him."

"Brandon chopped!" He held out the cutting board full of several dozen small fragments of cookie dough.

"Good job," Jane said to him. "You're the best chopper I've seen in a long time."

For a while no one spoke, as all three ate piece after piece of cookie dough.

"We'd better stop," Jane said then. "I'm starting to feel very abdominous."

"Me, too," Bethany said.

"Abtominous," Brandon said.

"Ab*d*ominous," Jane corrected.

"Abdominous," Brandon repeated happily.

Bethany wished Tavi's mother were there to hear him. *Abdominous* was one word she was willing to bet even Tavi, the wonder child, didn't know.

"So, anyway," Jane said, "what are we going to do about Donya's party?"

Bethany had known Jane would come back to that subject, sooner or later. "I don't want to go," Bethany said slowly.

"Let's not," Jane said. "Let's have—what do they call it?—a boycott. We'll boycott the party."

"But I think I pretty much have to go," Bethany went on. "If I don't, Donya's mother will tell my mother."

"So?"

So, what if Ms. Cabot said, "Bethany and Jane both refused to go to Donya's party. That Jane is really becoming a bad influence on Bethany, don't you think?" Bethany's mother would ask, "Jane who?" And Ms. Cabot would say, "Jane Owen," and Bethany's mother would say, "Wait a minute. Isn't she that girl who colors on wallpaper?"

"So?" was easy for *Jane* to say.

3
...

Bethany and Jane were in the same sixth-grade class at Mountainview Elementary School, on the south side of Pinevale. Their school really did have a view of the mountains: a steep, grassy slope began rising up to a sheer granite rock face directly behind the teachers' parking lot. Bethany liked that there were no mountains at all for two thousand miles, and then the Rocky Mountains soared up from the Colorado plains right at the edge of her own school parking lot. Sometimes deer gazed through the windows of the sixth-grade rooms, and then, plainly bored by math or social studies, quietly strolled away.

Bethany walked to school every day, but not with Jane. Jane liked to ride her bike to school, unless it was snowing too hard or the bike path was icy. "The better to make my getaway," Jane always said.

On Monday morning, Bethany arrived early. She waited for Jane near the bike racks. But Donya found her there first.

"Bad news," Donya said.

"What happened?" Bethany asked, to be polite. She knew from experience that Donya's bad news was never very bad, at least not from a normal person's perspective. For Donya, bad news was when her mother wouldn't let her buy the sweater she wanted at the mall, or when she copied a hairstyle from a magazine and it turned out funny.

"No boys."

Bethany didn't understand.

"At my *party*. My mother said I couldn't invite them. And my father backed her up. Can you believe it? I mean, he was a boy once. You'd think he'd want me to invite boys. But he says that's just the reason he doesn't want me to invite them. Because he was one, and so he knows how rowdy boys can be, and we just got new wall-to-wall carpet downstairs in the party room, and he thinks boys are more likely to spill."

Bethany tried to visualize Donya's problem on her problems list. She'd need a new ranking, for less than Not Serious. Maybe *R* for Ridiculous.

"You could tell them you'd only serve clear-colored sodas like 7UP and ginger ale," Bethany offered.

"I thought of that already. They still said no. So I don't think it's spilling they're really worried about. I think it's"—Donya lowered her voice—"kissing."

Bethany felt a rush of gratitude toward Donya's parents. If there was going to be kissing at Donya's party, she'd have to upgrade its seriousness on her own list to Very Serious.

"So it's definite?" Bethany asked her hopefully. "Definitely no boys? They're not going to change their minds?"

Donya shook her head. "The worst part is that I already told Doug and Matthew that I was going to invite them, and now I have to tell them they're uninvited. That's pretty rude. To invite someone one day and then take it back the next day."

"They'll understand," Bethany said. "It's not like it has anything to do with them personally."

It's not like inviting all the girls in our class except Nicole, and leaving her out just because she's a little bit chubby.

But Bethany didn't say it out loud. It was hard to tell someone right to her face that she was rude and unkind, especially someone who was supposed to be your best friend.

Jane coasted into the parking lot and braked beside the bike rack. Her short straight hair spiked out under the rim of her yellow helmet.

"Guess what?" Donya greeted her. "My parents said I can't invite boys, after all."

Jane pulled out a large white hankie from her vest pocket and pretended to weep. Then she stuffed the hankie away and took off her helmet.

"Did you ask your parents why they're being so antagonistic?" Jane asked.

"So what?"

"So opposed to having boys."

"They're parents," Donya said. "It's their job to be—that thing you just said."

"Antagonistic," Jane repeated.

"Anyway, they *are*, and so it's back to just the twelve of us."

"I think you should invite Nicole," Jane said.

Bethany almost felt jealous of Jane for saying so

easily what she hadn't been able to make herself say. She tried to look as if she weren't watching Donya's face for her response.

Donya shook her head. "Number one, my mother said twelve. You're the one who said she's antagonistic, not me. Number two, Nicole would not fit in. *She* wouldn't have a good time. Number three, we're going to have pizza, with a million different toppings. That has to be fattening, and Nicole's already so fat. Maybe she can't eat pizza, because she's supposed to be on a diet. Or maybe she'd eat two whole pizzas all by herself, and then there wouldn't be enough for everybody else."

"Bad reasons," Jane said. "Number one—"

The bell rang. Donya sprinted off to get in line.

"Number one," Jane said to Bethany, "it's mean. Number two, it's mean. Number three, it's mean."

"It *is* mean," Bethany said.

Saying it to Jane was easier than saying it to Donya.

At Mountainview, the sixth graders had their own wing of the school. Like the kids in junior high school, they changed classes, but they stayed with the same twenty-five kids, rotating as a group from one subject to the next. So Bethany was with Jane, Donya, and Nicole all day, moving from room to room according to the bell. After lunch, they went to the library for a half-period of study hall. Which meant that for twenty-five minutes every day they encountered Mr. Zucaro.

The last librarian, Ms. Levitt, had loved both children and books. But she had left in February to have a baby. Mr. Zucaro hated children. And Bethany was sure he hated books. He certainly didn't talk about books with any students at Mountainview Elementary School. Instead he talked about something he called "the noise level" in the library, and about how the sixth graders at Mountainview were the most disruptive children he had known in twenty years of being a school librarian.

That day Jane and Bethany didn't get seats together in the library. Jane sat at a table near the window with Donya and some of the boys; Bethany sat at the table near the computers, next to Nicole.

"There is no reason," Mr. Zucaro said, "that sixth graders should not be able to take their seats quietly. It doesn't require a great deal of conversation and discussion to locate an empty chair and seat yourself in it, now does it, Mr. Dogan?"

"No, sir," Doug Dogan muttered.

Mr. Zucaro liked to be called *sir*. It made being in study hall even more like being in boot camp. Not that Bethany had ever been in boot camp, but she had seen movies. Sergeants in boot camp made fresh-mouthed recruits do hundreds of push-ups. Mr. Zucaro made noisy students write essays with titles like "Respecting the Rights of Other Library Users."

"Now open your books," Mr. Zucaro said. "For the next twenty-five minutes, I don't want to hear any sound other than pages turning or pencils scratching."

That was another odd thing about Mr. Zucaro. Among the sounds he didn't want to hear were the sounds of students walking around the library, looking at books. The whole point of having study hall in the library was to encourage students to use it, but Mr. Zucaro frowned on students who left their seats to roam about from bookcase to bookcase.

When Nicole opened her book, Bethany saw that she had hidden a real book inside one of her Mountainview Elementary textbook covers—something called *The Once and Future King*.

Bethany caught Nicole's eye and gave her a quick grin, one that Mr. Zucaro couldn't see.

Bethany opened her social studies book and began reading the next assigned chapter, "Life in the Middle Ages." She read two paragraphs, but "Life in the Middle Ages" wasn't very exciting. Her eyelids began to feel heavy with sleep. It was hard, actually, to study in study hall.

"Miss Barrett," Mr. Zucaro hissed, close to her ear. "The library is not the place for an afternoon siesta. If you have an abnormal need for midday sleep, perhaps I should send you down to the school nurse for an examination."

"I'm fine," Bethany said, stifling a yawn. She tried to read the same two paragraphs over again. It would be fun to get out of study hall for the rest of the period, but what if the nurse ended up calling her mother? The last thing Bethany's mother needed was a phone call from Bethany's school.

"Miss McCloskey," Mr. Zucaro said to Nicole. Had he discovered that Nicole wasn't reading a schoolbook? "Let's not have any toe tapping. You can do your slimnastics before or after school, if you feel the need."

A wave of laughter swept over the class. The

thought of plump Nicole trying to lose weight by tapping her foot during study hall was a comical one. And only Mr. Zucaro would use a word like *slimnastics*. But the sarcastic meanness of the comment made Bethany flash an indignant look at Jane. She *did* abhor Mr. Zucaro; she really did.

Nicole flushed deep red, all the way down her neck to her T-shirt.

"Miss Cabot." Mr. Zucaro turned toward the window. "I hope that is not a note that you just passed to Miss Owen."

Donya, who'd been giggling with the others, now blushed herself. "No," she stammered. "It's not a note. It's just a question about the math homework. It really is."

"I'm sure it is," Mr. Zucaro said. "Miss Owen, please bring that piece of paper to me."

Bethany watched as Jane hesitated. Then slowly Jane came forward and handed Mr. Zucaro Donya's folded piece of paper, still unread. Was Mr. Zucaro going to read the note out loud? Bethany was sure it *was* a note, and she couldn't help hoping that it would be something embarrassing, something to do with boys.

" 'Dear Jane,' " Mr. Zucaro read in a high, mincing voice, apparently intended to sound like Donya's. " 'If you don't want to come to my party, that's fine with me. But don't tell me who to invite and who not to invite. I'm *not* inviting . . .' "

Mr. Zucaro's imitation of Donya trailed off. "Well," he said, "I am sure this will shed a great deal of light on your math homework, Miss Cabot."

Donya stared down at the table. Nicole nudged Bethany. "It's me, isn't it?" she whispered. "I heard some kids talking about Donya's party, but I haven't gotten an invitation for it yet. Have you?"

"Uh-huh. But—I'm not sure I'm going," Bethany said.

"Am I the only one she's not inviting?" Nicole asked.

"Miss Barrett, Miss McCloskey, I suppose you are discussing *your* math homework?"

Bethany turned back to "Life in the Middle Ages." Next to her, Nicole opened *The Once and Future King*. But she couldn't have been really reading it, because for the remaining fifteen minutes of study hall, Bethany never heard her turn a single page.

4
. . .

When Bethany arrived home from school, Brandon was out on the front porch, jumping on his trampoline. Brooke and her boyfriend, David, sat on the porch swing, watching him. Brooke and David were holding hands. Just like that, as if it were the most ordinary thing in the world to be sitting two inches away from a boy with your hand in his, your fingers intertwined with his fingers, *touching*.

Bethany wondered if her mother knew that Brooke and David were holding hands. Of course, Brooke was seventeen. She could hold hands with a boy if she wanted to. But Brooke's hand was right next to David's *leg*, tanned and hairy in his baggy shorts.

"No mail," Brooke said. "Not that I expected any. But I can't help looking, anyway."

By *mail*, Bethany knew Brooke meant college acceptance letters. Brooke had told her that they were never mailed until April fifteenth, still more than two weeks away. A thin envelope would mean a "no" letter; a thick envelope would mean a "yes," since with the letter of acceptance the college would send along all kinds of other information and forms to fill out. Sometimes Bethany had bad dreams about going to the mailbox and bringing in a thin envelope for Brooke from Yale or Cornell.

"Mom's inside working," Brooke said. "She has a real tight deadline, so David and I said we'd baby-sit for Brandon. How was school?"

"Okay."

"You're in the sixth grade, right?" David asked. He let go of Brooke's hand and draped his arm casually around her shoulders.

Bethany nodded.

"Sixth grade," David said with a nostalgic grin. "When I was in sixth grade, we had this teacher,

Mr. Teets. Every day he'd come into class and put his foot in the wastepaper can by the door and step on all the trash in it. He had this thing about packing the trash down with his foot. So one day my friend Alex and I took the wastepaper can to the boys' john before class and filled it halfway with water. Then we put the trash back in, so it would be kind of floating on top."

"You're kidding," Brooke said. "You didn't really."

"So when Teets came in, he stepped in the can as usual and got his pants leg wet to the knee."

"What did he do?" Bethany asked.

"Nothing. That was the strangest thing. It was as if he hadn't noticed. But after that he always took a yardstick and poked it in the can before he put his foot in it."

Brooke and Bethany couldn't help laughing. Nobody in their family would ever have done something like that to a teacher, something so funny—and awful.

"Oh, I have loads of Mr. Teets stories," David said.

Bethany sat down on the porch steps. "Lap," Brandon said. He left the trampoline and settled himself on Bethany's knees.

"Once, when he was showing our class a movie, he fell asleep. His head started bobbing, and he sat there swaying back and forth, with his mouth open so wide that a spitball could have shot right into it. So Alex and I, real quietly, got everyone to slip out of the room and to the playground, and when Teets woke up, the only kid who was left was this real goody-goody named Julia. Of course she told on us, and Alex and I caught it for that one. But it would have been great to see old Teets blinking and looking around and then gradually figuring out that everybody was gone. Too bad it was wasted on Julia."

David gave Brooke's shoulders a squeeze. "I bet you were like Julia, weren't you? The one kid who was never in trouble, Miss Smarty with all the right answers."

Brooke cuddled closer to David. Bethany could tell Brooke liked it when David teased her.

"Maybe a little bit," Brooke said. "But I think I would have left that day, too, if everyone else did. I mean, Mr. Teets shouldn't have fallen asleep. It was partly his fault, for sleeping on the job."

"Brandon want snack," Brandon said.

"I'll get it for him," Bethany told Brooke and David. She led Brandon into the kitchen.

The Mr. Teets stories had been funny, but it made Bethany nervous to be around so much lovey-doveyness. Brooke had only known David for a month. He was a year older than Brooke, already out of high school. He worked at the video store where the Barretts rented most of their movies. Once, at the store, he had started a conversation with Brooke about a movie she was returning, and he had asked her out on a movie date after that. And now every other sentence Brooke spoke was about David. David and college, college and David.

In the kitchen, Bethany poured milk for Brandon and put two graham crackers on a plate.

"Ice cream?" Brandon asked hopefully.

"Nope. It's too close to dinner. We don't have ice cream, anyway. All we have is orange sherbet."

Brandon broke into a laugh of pure delight.

"Sherbet?" Bethany asked. "You think that's a funny word—*sherbet?*"

The word set Brandon off again, with peals of laughter.

"I don't see what's so funny about *sherbet,*" Bethany said, emphasizing the word on purpose to make Brandon laugh again. "Many people find *sherbet* a very delicious snack. I myself am very fond of *sherbet*."

Brandon could hardly stop laughing.

"What's the joke?"

Bethany's mother appeared in the kitchen. Her eyes looked tired, the tiny wrinkles around the edges deeper than usual.

"I'm up to the *F* entries for *Europe in Transition*," she said wearily. "France: as African colonizer; immigration to; postwar economic problems of."

Bethany's mother worked at home as a freelance editor. Mostly she made indexes, for long, thick books with thousands of names in them. Halfway through an index she began to look pale and bleary-eyed, and sometimes she would talk in what their father called "index speak." They'd ask what was for dinner, and she'd say, "Beef, roast; potatoes, mashed; vegetables: see peas, green—frozen."

"Brandon and I were just talking about sherbet," Bethany said so that her mother could hear Brandon laugh again. Brandon certainly didn't sound slow or shy when he laughed. His laugh was so infectious that their mother joined in.

"Do you have any homework?" she asked Bethany when the laughter had subsided.

"Just my social studies report. The one that's due next week. And a few math problems."

"Is David still here?"

"They're on the porch."

"That's right; he said he didn't have to go to the store until six." Bethany's mother glanced at the kitchen clock. "I think sometimes David forgets that Brooke doesn't have the amount of free time that he does. When you're in the all-state orchestra, president of the French club, and have to study, too, you can't just sit around all day talking about which actor starred in which movie."

"David's nice," Bethany said, feeling suddenly defensive on Brooke's behalf.

"I didn't say he isn't. He's a very pleasant young man, and I'm sure he's thrilled to be dating someone like Brooke. But the fact remains that she has a lot of demands on her time, and I just hope—but of course she'll be going away to college next fall, so in any case . . ."

Halfway through an index, Bethany's mother sometimes had trouble finishing her sentences.

"Tiss," Brandon said.

"Tiss?" his mother asked. "This? What is this, honey? What do you want?"

"Tiss," Brandon repeated happily. "Book tiss."

Bethany's mother looked at her for help. "Which book?" she asked.

"He means Brooke," Bethany said. Brandon said *book* for *book* and for *Brooke*.

"Book tiss David," Brandon said.

Even Bethany's mother understood Brandon this time. Brandon pronounced his *K*'s like *T*'s.

The index worry lines deepened.

"That's nice," Ms. Barrett said automatically. But she went to the front door, and Bethany heard her say, "Brooke, honey, I think David had better be leaving pretty soon. You have a flute recital in a couple of weeks, and I don't think I've heard any practicing yet today."

Then Bethany's mother came back to the kitchen. Bethany noticed that she didn't get out Brandon's word book to write down word number 156: *kiss*.

David came over the next day, too, and the day after that. Bethany heard more Mr. Teets stories: about the time the boys hung Mr. Teets's big

"Battles of the Civil War" map out the second-story window and he spent the whole class period looking for it; about the time someone had seen Mr. Teets in the supermarket buying a bottle of men's Youthful Image hair dye.

On Thursday night, David came for supper. Bethany's father was home for supper, too, for the first time since the weekend. He traveled so much for his computer company that it seemed he was away more nights than he was home. Bethany's mother put aside her index and fixed a special, fancy beef stew for the occasion.

"The stew is great, Mom," Brooke said. "There's some different spice in here—cumin?"

Bethany couldn't eat it. She hated foods with strange spices in them. But she knew her mother had spent all afternoon cooking.

"I don't think Bethany likes it," her mother said, glancing at Bethany's practically untouched plate.

Before Bethany could think of a quick, polite lie, her father came to her rescue. "When I was in sixth grade, I didn't eat anything for a solid year but hamburgers, french fries, and Cokes. You couldn't have paid me to eat Middle Eastern beef stew."

Bethany flashed a grateful look at her dad. He

was the one who would take her side when her mother was nagging, or let Brooke skip flute practice, or pooh-pooh her mother's worries about Brandon's talking.

"You spend the first five years of your children's lives getting them to walk and talk," he liked to joke, "and then you spend the next fifteen years getting them to sit down and shut up." He called Brandon "the strong, silent type." "That's the type the girls all go for, eh, Brandon?" he'd say.

Bethany pretended to eat another forkful of stew. She couldn't help it if she didn't like the thought of raisins next to onions next to beef in a funny sauce. Brandon picked the raisins out of his stew with his fingers and left the beef. Brooke passed her plate forward for a second helping, and it seemed to Bethany that David had at least three helpings, maybe four. But she noticed that he didn't tell her parents any Mr. Teets stories.

After dinner Bethany closed the door to her room and slipped her problems list out of its hiding place. She had found a terrific *National Geographic* article on Afghanistan, so she crossed the social studies report off her list. It would be easy to do a good job on the report now. She still hadn't told her mother about the torn zipper on her jeans, but her mother would be done with her index by the weekend, and Bethany would tell her then.

Donya's party was getting closer all the time. Bethany knew that she would go—she *had* to go—but she still didn't *want* to. The memory of Nicole staring down at the unread page of her novel in study hall made Bethany squirm inside with a kind of guilt, even though she had never done a single thing to hurt Nicole's feelings.

What would it be like to be Jane and do or say whatever you wanted? Jane's parents were the same way. They were both college professors, and they didn't socialize with the other parents. Mr. Owen always wore jeans and a T-shirt in summer, jeans and a sweatshirt in winter. Every day Jane's mother wore the same blue jumper, only with a different-colored blouse, like a school uniform. She still had waist-long hair, even though it was mostly gray now, tied back in a ponytail by a rubber band or a piece of string or a shoelace.

It would be easier to be brave if your mother had a ponytail tied back with a shoelace.

Bethany turned to the hardest item on her list:

Brandon's talking. It was the same. At least she and Jane had learned seven new genius words: *antagonistic, aardwolf, abdominous, abhor, bamboozle, belligerent,* and *bombastic.* They had decided to move on to the *B*'s. As Jane had said, "A true genius doesn't limit herself to one letter of the alphabet." But so far Bethany couldn't say that her new vocabulary words had made much of a difference in anybody's life.

David had gone home, and from the room next door, Bethany could hear Brooke's stereo playing the same song over and over again: the theme song from the movie that had been the subject of Brooke and David's first conversation. It must be nice to be older, and to be a genius without even trying, and to have a boyfriend. Did Brooke have a problems list of her own? Bethany didn't think so. Sometimes she was sure she was the only person in the world with a problems list, and her list wasn't even complete: she hadn't made an entry yet for Middle Eastern beef stew.

5
...

"Would you do me a favor?" Bethany's mother asked Saturday afternoon, after Bethany's violin lesson. "I want to try to get this wretched index off to Federal Express by five o'clock today, and Brandon has a play date this afternoon with Tavi. Daddy's busy taking off the snow tires, and Brooke's off somewhere with David, of course. Would you walk him over there at two-thirty? You don't have to stay. His mom will call for us to get him when they're finished playing."

"Sure," Bethany said. She always felt cheerful when her lesson was over for the week. It was a good thing that she had decided to be a vocabulary genius rather than a musical genius. She would never play the violin as well as Brooke played the flute.

"Should I take anything? Besides bag, diaper?"

By the end of an index, all the Barretts, except Brandon, conversed in index speak.

"That's all. I'm up to Y, but unfortunately that still leaves Yugoslavia."

"At least there's no country in Europe that starts with a Z," Bethany said.

"True enough. But Y is going to be a doozy, with all those cross-references to Serbia and Slovenia and Croatia and Bosnia. Anyway, thank you, honey. The index for *Europe in Transition* is about to make a transition right out the door."

Bethany found Brandon in front of the TV in the family room, watching *Sesame Street*. She watched it with him for a while. Brandon could name every singing and dancing letter that came on the screen, even hard ones like Q. You had to be pretty smart to know the alphabet. Bethany wondered if Tavi knew all the upper- *and* lowercase letters, the way Brandon did.

Brandon had a poopy diaper, so Bethany changed him. Tavi was already toilet trained, but

Bethany knew a lot of three-year-olds who weren't. Rosa's brother Ian hadn't peed and pooped in the potty until he was almost four.

"Okay," Bethany told Brandon. "Let's go over to Tavi's house. Maybe you can play on his fire truck."

Brandon started for the door. "Brandon drive truck! Brandon ring bell!"

"Ding! Ding! Ding!" Bethany said. "It's a three-alarm fire, and Brandon Barrett, fire chief, is on the way!"

Tavi's family lived on the other side of Mountainview Elementary School, on the same steep street as Donya. On the way there, Bethany and Brandon passed a few brave daffodils struggling against the brisk April breeze. Pinevale was a windy town, especially in the spring.

On the front lawn of the school, a female deer sat silent in the sunlight, as still as if she were in a diorama at the museum of natural history. Her belly was swollen; Bethany knew that before too long there would be another baby fawn in the neighborhood to eat everybody's flowers.

Ms. Gordon opened the door as soon as Brandon knocked. She must have been watching for them from her front window.

"Bethany, Brandon, come in! Brandon, Tavi can't wait to see you. He's been talking about this play date ever since we set it up three days ago. Tavi!"

Tavi ran into the room, clutching his purple Barry Bear.

"Hi, Brandon," he said. "Do you want to go up-stairs and play with my new train?"

Brandon looked at Bethany.

"I bet he'd like to see your train later," Bethany said. "I think right now Brandon would love to play on your fire truck."

"Okay," Tavi said. "It's in the backyard. Come on, Brandon, let's go to my fire truck!"

Brandon ran after Tavi, his face full of excite-ment.

Bethany was conscious of Ms. Gordon watching the boys, listening to them, *noticing* that Brandon hadn't said a word since they arrived. But at home he had talked about wanting to ride Tavi's fire truck. How else would Bethany have known that he wanted to ride it? He was just shy at other peo-ple's houses, that was all.

"Would you like some fruit juice?" Ms. Gordon asked Bethany.

"No, thank you," Bethany said. "I can't stay. My mom said you'd call when Brandon was ready to go home."

"There're some fresh-baked oatmeal cookies to go with it."

"Well, I guess I could have one," Bethany said. She didn't want a cookie, but it seemed rude to refuse somebody's mother twice in a row.

Bethany followed Ms. Gordon to the kitchen.

"Sit down," Ms. Gordon said. "I'll have our snack ready in a minute."

Bethany perched on one of the tall white stools next to the counter dividing the kitchen from the breakfast nook. She could see the boys out the window, taking turns riding in Tavi's gleaming red fire engine. At least Tavi was good at taking turns. At Rosa and Ian's house, Brandon hardly ever got a turn unless Bethany stepped in and made the others share.

Ms. Gordon set a tall glass of orange juice and a plate with three oatmeal cookies on it in front of Bethany. Bethany took one cookie and nibbled at it.

"Brandon's always so quiet when he plays with Tavi," Ms. Gordon said, settling down with her mug of coffee on the stool next to Bethany's. "Is he that quiet at home, too?"

"No," Bethany said. She put the cookie back down on her plate. She felt as if she were being led into a trap. "I mean, he's quiet, but he *talks*."

"Does he talk in sentences?"

"Uh-huh," Bethany said. Brandon drive truck. Brandon ring bell. Didn't those count as sentences?

"When I've heard him, he usually talks in single words or phrases, and what sentences he says are short and choppy."

Bethany felt her cheeks flushing. "A lot of children don't talk much," she said. "Einstein didn't—"

"—talk until he was four." Ms. Gordon finished Bethany's sentence for her. "That's what everyone whose child is delayed in language development says. But that kind of attitude doesn't do anything to help the child in question."

"Brandon knows the whole alphabet," Bethany said. "Capital letters *and* small ones."

Ms. Gordon looked surprised. Bethany felt that she had scored a point. Tavi must not know his letters yet.

"That's nice," she said, looking as if she didn't believe it. "But developmentally, what's important for Brandon right now is oral language—everyday conversation."

So what was Bethany supposed to do about it? If she could make him talk, she would.

"I don't mean to put any pressure on you, Bethany," Ms. Gordon said. "I just get the feeling that your mother doesn't want to accept that Brandon may have a learning disability. I've tried to talk to her, but she cuts me off, as if I'm interfering."

As if.

Bethany didn't say anything. She was afraid she might start crying if she tried to speak.

"What's new with you, dear?" Ms. Gordon asked then, obviously finished with the subject of Brandon. "And with Brooke? She'll be hearing from colleges any day now, I expect. I hope she won't be too disappointed if she doesn't get into her first choice. Those East Coast schools are highly competitive these days, and all the applicants are top students."

Bethany had to leave. She couldn't bear another minute of Ms. Gordon. She abhorred Ms. Gordon as much as she abhorred Mr. Zucaro.

"I forgot—" she said in a strangled voice. "I have to go right away. I promised my mother I wouldn't stay."

"Here, let me wrap up those cookies for you."

Bethany shook her head.

"Okay, dear. I'll call when Brandon is ready to go. It was so nice to have a little visit with you."

Outside, Bethany started running. The tears she had struggled to hold back at Tavi's house streamed down her face. She didn't stop until she had reached Jane's tree fort.

Jane wasn't there, but Bethany climbed up into the fort, anyway. She pored over the rest of the *B*'s in Jane's dictionary, and twenty pages of *C*'s, until she found a good word to describe Ms. Gordon: *captious*—"fond of catching others in mistakes, quick to find fault, quibbling, carping." Under *carp*, the dictionary said, "to complain or find fault in a petty or nagging way."

"Ms. Gordon is just a captious woman who likes to carp," Bethany informed the neighboring squirrel. She felt better then, calm enough to go home and face her mother as if nothing had happened.

"Ouch!" Bethany yelped.

"I'm almost done," Donya said. "Hold still for just another minute."

Bethany clenched her teeth as Donya's fingers continued twisting her hair. "Ouch!" she said again.

Donya gave a final twist. "They're finished!"

Donya swung Bethany's chair around so that she could see her new French braids in Donya's bedroom mirror. They gave a sleek, elegant look to Bethany's shoulder-length, soft brown hair.

"Wear your hair that way to my party," Donya

offered. "Come over a little bit early, and I'll make them for you again."

"Maybe," Bethany said. The braids did look beautiful, but it had taken Donya almost fifteen minutes to do them, and Bethany's scalp felt sore and tight from the pressure.

"It won't take me so long next time," Donya said.

Bethany was spending Sunday afternoon at Donya's house. She had to go there sometimes, or she couldn't even pretend to be Donya's friend. And sometimes Bethany liked Donya, in spite of everything. She liked her right now, while they sipped ice-cold diet Cokes in Donya's girly-girl bedroom, just the two of them alone, without Donya's real best friend, Evie, who was worse by far than Donya. There was something safe and re-assuring about Donya. Bethany's mother liked her. The teachers at school liked her, except for Mr. Zucaro, who didn't like anybody. All the other girls at school liked her, except for Jane.

"Have you finished your country report?" Donya said then.

"Almost."

"How long is it?"

"I guess it'll be about fifteen pages, including the index and the bibliography."

"Mine is only eleven," Donya said. "But there isn't a lot to say about China. Who's that guy that Brooke is with all the time?"

"Her new boyfriend. David. He's nice."

"He's *cute*," Donya said. "Like, with a capital *C*. Does Brooke tell you things?"

"What kind of things?"

"You know, about kissing boys. What it's like to do it. Like, how far do you open your mouth, and how long is the first kiss supposed to last, and how, like, wet should it be."

"No," Bethany said.

"You should ask her," Donya said. "I wish I had an older sister. I mean, what if my parents *had* let me invite boys to my party? How are we supposed to know these things if nobody tells us?"

"I don't know," Bethany said. But she couldn't even imagine having a conversation about kissing with Brooke. She loved Brooke, and she knew Brooke loved her, but she and Brooke didn't really talk very often—certainly not about how far you opened your mouth when you kissed a boy, or even about who you were really best friends with while you pretended to be best friends with someone else.

"There should be a book," Donya said. "*Kissing: the Truth, the Whole Truth, and Nothing but the Truth.*"

"Maybe there's one in the school library," Bethany suggested, teasing.

"Let's ask Mr. Zucaro!" both girls said in the same instant, and dissolved into spasms of hysterical laughter.

Bethany didn't need a book about kissing. She needed a different kind of book, a book about talking—a book that would tell you how much you were supposed to be talking when you had just turned three, and how bad it was if you weren't talking that much yet.

On Monday, during study hall, Bethany forced herself to raise her hand. "May I use the computer catalog?" she asked politely.

Mr. Zucaro frowned. "I suppose so," he said. "This *is* for a school report, isn't it?"

"Yes," Bethany lied.

"Five minutes," Mr. Zucaro said as Bethany sat down in front of the computer. "I want you back in your seat in five minutes."

"But after I find the book in the catalog, I need to find it on the shelf," Bethany said.

Mr. Zucaro sighed, implying that it was a great burden to deal with the unreasonable requests of sixth graders all day long. "Ten minutes," he said.

Bethany wasted her first minute at the computer, wondering what subject headings she should use. *Talking* didn't sound fancy enough. *Speech?* The Mountainview Elementary School library didn't have any books on speech. What word had Ms. Gordon used? *Language development.* Nothing on language development, either. *Development, language.* Ah-ha! Not for nothing was Bethany an indexer's daughter. There were three books on development, child: one by Dr. Spock and two by people Bethany had never heard of.

Silently, stealthily, Bethany tiptoed over to the shelf with the books on it. She had to admit that Mr. Zucaro's scowling presence added a certain guilty thrill to library research. She found the books right away and flipped knowledgeably through the indexes to find the pages she wanted.

Dr. Spock was the most reassuring. He made it seem as if perfectly normal toddlers talked late all the time. He implied that it was no big deal if a child talked late. In Bethany's favorite sentence, Dr. Spock said that most late talkers had normal intelligence, and some of them were "unusually bright."

So there, Ms. Gordon!

The second book was also comforting. It said that children developed language at different rates for different reasons. It said that one child might talk less than another because he was a boy, or because he had talkative older siblings who didn't give him a chance to talk. Brandon was a boy, with two older sisters. Of course, Tavi was a boy, too, but Tavi was an only child. The book said to worry if a child wasn't talking *at all* by the time he was two-and-a-half, but Brandon was definitely talking. He knew 165 words. Bethany had checked the list that morning. And he did speak in sentences lots of times, no matter what Ms. Gordon said.

But the third book could have been written by Ms. Gordon herself. It had a little timetable, year by year, month by month, telling everything that a normal child should be doing by each age. It said that the typical child of three would have a vocabulary of several hundred words. One hundred sixty-five wasn't several hundred. It said the typical child would use pronouns: *I, you, he, she*. Brandon hardly ever used pronouns. It said the typical child would talk in tenses: *I go, I went, I will go*. Brandon didn't use tenses. According to the chart, Brandon was more like the typical two-year-old.

"Miss Barrett." The voice came from behind Bethany, startling her. "You have been standing here for fifteen minutes, by my watch."

"I'm *studying*." Bethany was surprised by the fierceness in her own voice. "This is study hall, and I am studying."

"Delayed speech development?" Mr. Zucaro read from the book Bethany had left lying open on the shelf. "I hardly think that anyone in this class needs to worry about insufficient quantity of talking."

Bethany knew this was Mr. Zucaro's standard sarcasm, like his crack to Nicole about slimnastics. But she was so angry that she almost said something back, something so cruel and terrible that Mr. Zucaro would never forget it as long as he lived:

You have a whiny high voice like a mosquito.

Everybody in this school hates you.

You are the worst librarian I have ever met in my whole entire life.

Bethany didn't say anything. She left the books where they were and took her seat.

After school, Bethany caught up with Jane at the bike racks. "I wrote a poem," she said. "About Mr. Zucaro. In math, while Ms. Harper was reviewing for the test."

"Let's see it," Jane said.

Helmet in hand, Jane stood and read Bethany's poem aloud in a grand style, as if she were a famous actor on the Broadway stage:

Ode to Mr. Zucaro in Springtime

This library is a place to work.
Don't sit there grinning like a fool.
Spit out your gum and shut your mouth,
And do your slimnastics after school.

Give me that note. Your private mail
Is for me to read to all.
Don't talk. Don't move. Don't even think.
How dare you think in study hall?

I'm talking to you, Miss So-and-so.
Perhaps the doctor should check your ears.
The twenty-five minutes you study here
Only seem like twenty-five years.

Smiling is against the rules.
Wipe that smirk right off your face.
And whatever you do, don't touch the books.
ISN'T OUR LIBRARY A PLEASANT PLACE?!

Jane looked at her solemnly when she had finished. "Bethany," she said, "forget the dictionary. Forget long words. You *are* a genius."

"Do you like it?" Bethany asked.

"Like it? This should be published. You should read it on National Public Radio. Schoolchildren the world over should have to memorize it. Can I have a copy? I want to show it someday to my grandchildren."

"You can keep this one," Bethany said. "I know it by heart."

Maybe she *could* be a genius. Jane's praise made her feel like turning cartwheels—although Donya would have to teach her how to do one first.

7
...

"How was school today, honey?"

"Fine."

"Did you write any brilliant satiric poems about that horrible Mr. Zucaro?"

"Not really. I mean—as a matter of fact, well, yes."

But that wasn't how the conversation went. After asking how school had been and hearing Bethany's "Fine," her mother looked relieved and began rummaging in the diaper bag for sunblock to put on Brandon.

Should Bethany tell her about the poem, any-

69

way? It wasn't every day that she wrote a work of poetic genius. Jane told things all the time to *her* mother; she was probably reading Bethany's poem to *her* mother right that very minute. But Bethany knew she wouldn't launch into the whole complicated story about Mr. Zucaro and his meanness. It wasn't her mother's kind of story, that was all. Her mother's kind of story would be a story about how Bethany and Donya had shared an award for being the best library helpers.

"Do you want to come to the grocery store with Brandon and me?" Bethany's mother asked then. "The cupboard is bare."

"Sure," Bethany said.

On the way to the grocery store, they passed David and Brooke driving home. David honked and waved. Bethany waved back, but her mother didn't. "Oh, dear," she said. "Maybe we should— but we do need groceries. We can't order in pizza every night. But I hope . . ."

Sometimes even after an index was finished, Bethany's mother talked in incomplete sentences. Bethany wasn't sure she wanted her mother to finish that sentence, anyway.

"I guess you just do all you can to bring up your

children and instill your values in them, and then you hope for the best," Bethany's mother said, turning in to the King Soopers parking lot. "Brooke knows what we expect of her. I just wonder . . . with all those academically minded high school boys—musicians, too—who share her interests . . ."

Bethany knew the end of that sentence: why did Brooke pick David? She thought she knew the answer, too: because David wasn't another academically minded high school musician who shared Brooke's interests.

"Brooke and David both like movies," Bethany said.

"*Movies.*" Her mother said it as if sharing an interest in movies was worse than sharing an interest in nothing at all.

"She hardly sees her girlfriends anymore, either. That nice Martha and Jamie, with the harp. Oh, Bethany, I saw Katie Cabot at the library this afternoon, and she told me that Donya is planning quite the birthday party. She was surprised that I didn't know all about it."

"It's this Saturday," Bethany said.

"So Katie told me. I'm glad I don't have to depend on my own daughter for information about the most exciting events of the sixth-grade social season."

Her mother gave her a quick grin, so Bethany knew that she was—mostly—teasing. But she could also hear the pride in her mother's voice that her daughter was one of the popular girls, someone who got invited to the important parties given by other popular girls. She probably should have mentioned Donya's party sooner. She had just hoped that somehow it would turn out that she didn't really have to go.

At King Soopers, the cart filled up quickly with bread, milk, yogurt, fruit, cans of tuna and beans.

"That's another thing," Bethany's mother said, as much to herself as to Bethany. "The quantity that David eats! I think he saves on his grocery bill by loading up on snacks at our house. I mean it. Half a leftover pizza is like a handful of popcorn to him."

"Popcorn?" Brandon asked from his seat in the front of the shopping cart. "Brandon want popcorn."

"Okay, let's get some microwave popcorn. It's in aisle six," Bethany's mother said to her. "Get whatever brand's cheapest."

Bethany came back with the popcorn as her mother was turning in to the checkout line.

"Thank you, honey. Now for the bad news." Bethany's mother opened her wallet and took out her credit card.

"Brandon do it." Brandon reached for the card. "Brandon pay."

The woman at the register took the card from him with a friendly grin. "You're a cutie," she said. "How old are you?"

Brandon didn't answer.

"Are you three?"

"Almost. He'll be three in a couple of months," Bethany's mother said. "One hundred and forty dollars! I guess I knew it would be high this time."

Bethany stared. Brandon was already three. His party had been just a week ago. Her mother couldn't have forgotten Brandon's party—the party with the wrong balloons. Had she answered absentmindedly, out of habit? Bethany didn't think so.

"Do you need any help to the car?" the checkout woman asked.

"No, thank you," Bethany's mother said. "I have my two best helpers with me."

Her mother's voice sounded light and natural, but Bethany knew, as certainly as she knew anything, that her mother hadn't made a mistake about Brandon's age. Her mother had lied. She had lied to make it seem less bad that Brandon didn't talk more.

At school the next day, Bethany handed in her report on Afghanistan. She took a test in science. Bethany was good at science, so the test had never made it onto her problems list. In gym class they went outside to start softball. Bethany wasn't good at softball, but striking out at softball wasn't a problem, really. It was just a fact of life. When Ms. Kohler let the girls pick teams, Bethany was never chosen first, unless Jane was the one choosing. But she wasn't chosen last, either: Nicole was chosen last.

That day they didn't play a real softball game. They took turns throwing and catching and hitting. Bethany threw worse than she hit, and caught worse than she threw. Jane wasn't very good, either, but Jane was in the mood to pretend she cared. So before every pitch Jane went through an elaborate windup, and before she got up to bat, she rubbed the bat with dirt so that her hands wouldn't slip and tried out different grips. When she struck out, Jane acted as if she were overcome with misery.

"That's enough, Jane," Ms. Kohler said.

Nicole wasn't much worse than Bethany, actually, but there was something about Nicole that made even Bethany want to laugh when Nicole took a turn. Nicole didn't just strike out: she swung so wide of the mark that it was comical. She didn't just miss catching a ball: she threw her mitt up in front of her face and squealed. And—Bethany hated to think it—be it *was* funnier when a plump person threw the ball so wildly. Nicole's shorts and T-shirt were too small for her, so a roll of soft tummy peeked out in between. Tummies were funny. They just were.

"Nicole!" Evie shouted. "Pardon me, but your epidermis is showing."

Epidermis, Bethany knew, was a genius word for *skin.* It was a joke to tell someone that her epidermis was showing, because everybody's epidermis showed all the time, at least the part of it that covered your face and your hands.

Nicole looked flustered and tugged down on her

shirt where it gaped above her tummy.

When it was Evie's turn to throw the ball to Nicole, she called out, "Hey, Tums!"

Of course everyone giggled, except for Bethany and Jane.

Ms. Kohler frowned. "Evelyn, please throw the ball to *Nicole*."

Evie threw it, but she was laughing so hard that the ball hit the ground short of Nicole, so Nicole didn't have to hide her face and squeal.

How did nicknames spread so quickly? In math class that afternoon, two boys called Nicole Tums. And the next day, when Nicole went to take her seat in English class, there was a roll of Tums antacid tablets with calcium lying in the middle of her desk. Nicole didn't cry when she saw it, but her face turned so red that it looked like a red balloon.

During study hall Doug Dogan, sitting next to Nicole, began to chant, like a Tums commercial, "Tums, Tums, Tums, Tums."

Now Nicole looked like a purple balloon.

"There will be no singing in this library," Mr. Zucaro said sharply, whirling around to pounce on the singer. He looked over at Nicole's table, and seeing her flushed face, took her for the guilty party. "Miss McCloskey, I hardly think the Tums company is paying you to advertise their products."

The laughter that greeted this remark was so boisterous that Mr. Zucaro hid a small smile. For once Mr. Zucaro must have felt like one of the popular teachers, whose cracks kept kids laughing. But in an instant he regained control of himself.

"There will be no singing *or* laughing. Please resume your silent study."

After school, Bethany couldn't wait to find Jane and talk with her about how awful everyone was being to Nicole, especially Evie and Mr. Zucaro and the boys, but Donya, too. Bethany suspected that Donya had brought in the roll of Tums. She knew Donya's mother took a Tums every day for the calcium. Bethany didn't think Donya herself would have put the Tums on Nicole's desk, but she might have given them to Evie and let Evie do it. That would be just like an aardwolf.

When Bethany reached the bike rack, Jane grabbed her arm. "Nicole's coming out right now. Is it okay if we invite her to the tree fort?"

Bethany swallowed hard. She felt sorry for Nicole. She hated the others for teasing Nicole. And she *liked* Nicole. It would be fun to find out

what *The Once and Future King* was all about. But
she didn't particularly want to be *friends* with
Nicole. It was dangerous enough being friends
with Jane. And she and Jane had never invited
anyone else to their secret tree fort.

What could Bethany say?

"Okay."

With that one word, Bethany felt as if a line
were being drawn between the popular kids on
one side, and Nicole, Jane, and her on the other.
And her mother would want her to stay on Donya's
side of the line.

"Nicole!" Jane called after her. "Come here a
minute! Bethany and I have something we want to
ask you."

It was hard getting Nicole up to the tree fort.
Nicole was no better at climbing than she was at
catching softballs, and when she first saw the
skinny rope ladder leading all the way up to the
fort, she gave a little gasp.

"I can't," Nicole said. "You and Bethany were
great to invite me, and your fort looks really terrific, but I can't climb a ladder like that. I can't."

"Sure you can," Jane said. "Bethany'll go first, so

you can see how to do it, and I'll come up right behind you."

Somehow Nicole did it, although she was almost crying with fear and relief when she reached the top.

"Ta-dah," Jane said. "This is it. This is where Bethany and I spy."

"Who do you spy on?" Nicole asked, settling herself as far from the door as possible.

"On our enemies," Jane said. "And on our friends."

Nicole picked up Jane's dictionary. "What's this for?" she asked.

Jane looked over at Bethany. The genius plan belonged to Bethany. Jane knew it was *her* decision whether or not to share it.

Oh, well.

"Jane and I are learning really fancy words," Bethany explained. "We go through the dictionary and pick out great new words to use. It's kind of like a way of becoming . . . geniuses."

It sounded silly when she said it.

"We're only up to *B*," she added.

"Can I play, too?" Nicole asked. "I have a book at home, called a thesaurus, and it tells you all kinds of words that mean the same thing. Like, say you want to know a lot of words that all mean *obnoxious*. Like if you want to describe—"

"Mr. Zucaro," Bethany said.

"Right. So you'd look up *obnoxious* in my book, and it would say, *repugnant, repulsive, noisome, revolting, offensive.*"

Bethany could tell that Nicole must have looked up *obnoxious* quite often.

"I like it," Jane said. "It describes him exactly. Somebody ought to do something obnoxious to *him*, something so revolting and offensive that he'll never dare be obnoxious to us again. Bring your book next time you come."

"Okay," Nicole said. "I mean, if you want me to come again."

Bethany tried not to hear the longing in Nicole's voice. She flipped on through the *B*'s in Jane's dictionary. "Look, here's another good one. *Bravura.* 'A bold display of daring; dash.' "

"Nicole, you climbed the ladder with bravura," Jane tried.

"No, I didn't. I climbed it with terror."

"Well, next time you'll climb it with bravura."

Three heads bent over the dictionary. *Brawny.*

Brazen. Brinkmanship. The last one was Bethany's favorite of the day. *Brinkmanship*: "The policy of pursuing a hazardous course of action to the brink of catastrophe." She couldn't think of a sentence to use it in, but she would someday.

Bethany had to admit that Nicole fit in, that Nicole would make a good fellow genius. But if she became friends with Nicole, it was hard to see how she could stay friends with Donya. You couldn't be friends both with someone who was left out of a party and with the person who had left her out.

Now Bethany's mother would have one child who didn't talk and one who had the wrong kind of boyfriend and one who had the wrong kind of girl-friends. If Bethany really wanted to help her mother by being perfect, this was not the way to do it.

8
...

*T*he library at Mountainview Elementary School was located in the very center of the school, next to the school offices, so that you had to walk by it on the way to anywhere else. The bulletin board outside the library was the place that the principal and school staff posted all important announcements and achievements. Usually Bethany didn't stop to read them. Announcements about resurfacing the school parking lot or examples of outstanding second-grade artwork weren't important to her. So she hardly knew why an ordinary sheet of notebook paper tacked up there the next morning caught her attention as she walked past it on the way to first-period English.

It was probably because out of the corner of her eye she could see it was a poem. Bethany couldn't remember ever seeing a poem on the central school bulletin board. It was worth stopping to read a poem.

But one glance at the poem was enough. As soon as Bethany saw Mr. Zucaro's name in the title, it was enough.

"This library is a place to work. . . ."

Bethany reached to yank it down, to tear it into a million little pieces before Mr. Zucaro could see it, when suddenly Mr. Shapiro, the social studies teacher, was beside her.

"Good work on Afghanistan," he said.

Bethany couldn't very well rip an announcement off the school bulletin board with a teacher watching.

"I won't be able to give the reports back until next week," Mr. Shapiro went on, "but I started reading them last night. Yours is very nice, although maybe you rely too much on that one article from *National Geographic*."

"I had trouble finding any books," Bethany said.

"Come on, I'll walk to the south wing with you," Mr. Shapiro said. Reluctantly, Bethany followed him down the now-empty corridor.

"You even had an index," Mr. Shapiro said. "You were the only student to include an index."

"My mother is an indexer," Bethany said.

"Ah-ha. That explains it."

They were outside the social studies room now, but Mr. Shapiro didn't seem ready to stop talking. "In fact, I've been teaching for going on twenty years—nineteen years, this June—and I don't believe I've ever had a student include an index with his or her report."

The bell rang.

"Keep up the good work," Mr. Shapiro said, and finally turned in to his classroom. Did Bethany have time to run back to the bulletin board? Was it worse to be late to English class or to leave "Ode to Mr. Zucaro in Springtime" displayed for the whole school—and Mr. Zucaro—to see?

Bethany sprinted toward the library, her stomach churning with fear and, worse than fear, a new kind of rage. For Jane had to be the one who had posted the poem on the bulletin board. Jane had the only copy of it. For the first time in all their years of secret friendship, Bethany was furious with Jane. Jane had no right to do what she had done. She had no right!

"No running, please."

Right there, not two feet from the bulletin board, stood Mr. Ryan, the school principal, scanning the hallway for latecomers.

Bethany stopped abruptly. The principal looked more closely at Bethany.

"You're a sixth grader. Don't you belong in the south wing of the building?"

"Yes, but—I dropped one of my books, and I was going back to get it."

"Where did you drop it?"

"I don't know for sure. I think—outside, by the bike racks."

"All right," Mr. Ryan said. "Go out to check, but if it's not there, come right back in. I don't want you traipsing all over the school lot looking for it."

Bethany went out to the bike racks. Her book wasn't there, which was hardly surprising.

"Did you find it?" Mr. Ryan asked when Bethany slowly walked back inside the school.

Obviously not. Bethany was empty-handed.

"You might inquire at the lost-and-found in the

85

school office later in the day," Mr. Ryan suggested.

Lost: one satiric poem. Found: in the worst possible location in the whole school.

"Now hurry on back to class," Mr. Ryan said, and he watched her as she went.

During English class, Bethany didn't let herself even look at Jane. She was so angry that one look might become a laser beam that would shrivel Jane to a heap of flimsy gray ash. By the time class had ended, Bethany's anger had cooled enough that her hands didn't shake as she gathered up her textbooks. But she still wished she had never been friends with Jane.

What could you expect from someone who would color on someone else's new zoo wallpaper?

She wondered if Mr. Zucaro had read the poem yet.

Jane caught up with Bethany in the hallway between classes. "Did you see it?" she asked.

"See what?" Bethany spat out the words.

"Your poem. I had a brainstorm last night, after you left. Our perfect revenge on Mr. Zucaro! I copied it over, nice and neat, and put it up on the bulletin board in front of the library. After he made that crack yesterday about Nicole working for the Tums company, he deserves it."

Bethany didn't say anything.

"I didn't put your name on it," Jane said. "I mean, you deserve full credit for being a literary genius, but I knew it was better not to. . . ." Jane's voice trailed off. "I would have called to ask, but I didn't want your mom to answer, and when I got here this morning you were with Donya. . . . You're not—you look like you're mad or something."

Bethany whirled around. "Of course I'm mad. That was *my* poem. You had no right. You can't just take someone else's poem and stick it up like that for the whole world to see."

"But, Bethany." Jane clearly didn't understand. "It's a wonderful poem. It really is."

"Mr. Zucaro's going to know who wrote it," Bethany said. "It's obviously me. He's going to find out, and he's not going to laugh and shrug it off. You know he's not."

"First of all, he's not going to find out," Jane said. "And second of all, even if he does, so what? You can't put someone in jail for writing a poem. He can't expel us. The worst that could happen would be detention or something. Or calling our parents."

Bethany was afraid she was going to cry right in the hallway outside Mr. Shapiro's room. Somehow she swallowed back the tears, like a gulp of thick, foul-tasting medicine.

Teachers never called Bethany's parents, except to announce some special summer program that Brooke had been accepted into, or a science-fair award that Brooke had won. Bethany wanted teachers to start calling her parents for special genius programs that *she* had been accepted into and vocabulary prizes that *she* had won. If the school called because of her Mr. Zucaro poem, it would be worse than all the other problems on her list put together.

Once in the third grade, Bethany had gotten a B on her report card in "Cooperation with Others," and when she had made herself show it to her mother, her mother had cried. Her mother would never get over a phone call from Mr. Zucaro. It would be like getting an F in "Cooperation with Others."

But Bethany couldn't stay angry with Jane. She knew that Jane had only meant to punish Mr.

Zucaro. Jane hadn't meant to punish *her*.

When Bethany and Jane passed the library on the way to lunch, the poem was gone. The question was: Had it been taken down before or after Mr. Zucaro had seen it?

Bethany didn't have to wait long to find out. In study hall, directly after lunch, Mr. Zucaro stood in silence as the students took their seats. Then he began to speak. "It appears that we have a *poet* among us," he said. He said *poet* the way someone else might say *ax murderer*.

From his desk he picked up Jane's sheet of notebook paper, holding it with two fingers as if he didn't want to soil his hands with its filth. "Would the author of 'Ode to Mr. Zucaro in Springtime' be so kind as to identify himself or herself to me?"

No one raised a hand. Bethany was sure Mr. Zucaro could hear her pounding heart two tables away.

"Very well, then. Would each of you please take a piece of paper from your notebook. Then take out your pens. I want you to write down two sentences, exactly as I read them to you. Use cursive writing. Do not print. Are you ready? 'This library is a place to work. / Don't sit there grinning like a fool.' "

The lines should have made the class laugh. No one so much as smiled.

Bethany copied the lines. She thought about trying to disguise her handwriting, but there was no point in it. It was Jane, not Bethany, who needed to disguise her writing. Of course, the original of the poem was in Bethany's handwriting, but she planned to destroy it the instant they reached Jane's tree fort after school.

Jane was seated across from Bethany. Jane looked pale and tense. It would be tricky to disguise your handwriting so that nobody could recognize it. The easiest way would be to print instead of write, but Mr. Zucaro had specifically said he wanted cursive writing.

Mr. Zucaro walked around the room collecting the samples.

"Thank you," he said when he had placed the pile in front of himself on his desk. "You may resume your silent study."

Bethany tried to study, or at least to pretend she was studying, but it was all she could do to keep her eyes focused on the page in front of her. She didn't dare look at Mr. Zucaro, but she knew he was sitting at his desk, sifting through the handwriting samples, comparing each one to the handwriting of the poem.

At last, study hall was over. If Mr. Zucaro had recognized the writing, he didn't let on.

Bethany and Jane didn't say another word to each other about the poem until they were in Jane's tree fort, just the two of them, with the rope ladder pulled up behind them. Even then they whispered.

"Whew!" Jane said. "What a scary guy."

"Do you think—what did you do about your writing, so he wouldn't know it was you?"

"Well, I wrote extra neat for the bulletin board, so for the sample I wrote extra messy. And usually I write pretty big, so on the sample I made my writing really small."

"Do you have the other copy of the poem? My copy?"

"It's right here." Jane opened her treasure box and took out a folded sheet of paper.

"I want to burn it," Bethany said. "Do your parents have any matches?"

"Don't," Jane said. "It really is a work of genius.

You shouldn't burn it up. It's safe here. Mr. Zucaro isn't going to search people's *houses*. No one knows about the tree fort but us."

"And Nicole."

"She'll never come here unless she's with us. She's not going to climb that ladder all by herself. Besides, I think we can trust Nicole," Jane said.

"I thought—" Bethany had a sudden lump in her throat. "I thought I could trust *you*."

Jane didn't say anything for a moment. Bethany's words hung in the air.

"I'm sorry," Jane said then in a low voice. "Bethany, I really truly am sorry. And look, I'm the one he's after, not you. It's my handwriting he's trying to match. And if he finds out it was me, I'll never breathe a word about you. Even if he tortures me on the rack, I won't utter a syllable of your name."

Jane reached for Bethany's hand. Bethany let her hold it.

"But you know what I wish?" Jane asked then. "I wish he had made us copy the whole thing. I wish he had read aloud the whole entire poem for us to copy."

"I wish I had never written it," Bethany said.

That was the biggest difference between Bethany and Jane. Jane liked brinkmanship. She liked pursuing hazardous courses of action to the brink of catastrophe. Bethany didn't.

9

...

All through the afternoon and evening, Bethany waited for a knock on her door: it would be Mr. Zucaro, announcing to her parents that their daughter was the author of "Ode to Mr. Zucaro in Springtime." Whenever the phone rang, she sat in an agony of dread until she found out that it wasn't Mr. Zucaro or Mr. Ryan. *This* time.

Surely Mr. Zucaro must be collecting other evidence against her, or against Jane. There was the poem itself. The line about slimnastics might implicate Nicole—or Bethany, who had sat next to her

94

that day, whispering. The line about reading other people's mail pointed to Donya, the author of the note, or to Jane, its intended recipient, or to Bethany, who was sure she had flinched visibly when it was read aloud. On the other hand, "Don't sit there grinning like a fool" pointed to Doug Dogan, the boy Mr. Zucaro usually yelled at for smiling.

When Bethany went into the library on Friday, she wondered if Mr. Zucaro would produce a little ink pad and begin collecting everybody's fingerprints. There was no way Jane could disguise those. But he didn't. He was colder than ever, and there was some icy fire in his eyes that made everybody sit down quietly and study in silence.

Mr. Zucaro didn't make any more sarcastic quips to the class. Bethany didn't know if it was because everyone was so well behaved, or because the poem had shown Mr. Zucaro the truth about how mean he was.

All day long, in every break between classes, the others asked about the poem—who had written it, what it had said. Nicole didn't ask; Bethany had a feeling that Nicole knew.

Jane, too, kept resolutely quiet during all discussions about the poem. Actually, that was probably the single best reason for the others to suspect that Jane had more to do with the poem than she was saying. Jane's silence was practically a public admission of guilt.

After school on Friday, when they were at Donya's house making final preparations for the party on Saturday night, Donya asked Bethany right out. "You can tell me," Donya said suddenly, looking up from her stack of CDs. "I won't tell; I promise. Was it Jane? Was Jane the one who wrote the poem about Mr. Zucaro?"

"No," Bethany said. She bent her head to examine the back of one of Donya's CDs.

"You're sure it wasn't Jane?"

"Uh-huh."

"Then—well, I don't think it was one of the boys. Most boys don't write poetry. Could it have been Tums? Mr. Zucaro always picks on her."

So do you and Evie. And her name is *Nicole*.

"Maybe," Bethany said. "I don't think so." She hated herself for letting the cruel nickname go by another time. She didn't know how she could have done it, after the good time she had shared with Nicole in the tree fort. But she did.

"I don't think so, either. She doesn't have enough nerve."

Bethany didn't say anything.

"That's why it has to be Jane. She's the only one nervy enough. Unless it was someone in another study hall. There *are* four sixth-grade study halls. But couldn't you just feel it in the air this week? Didn't it feel like it was one of us?"

"All the other study halls probably felt like it was one of them," Bethany said. "I'm sure Mr. Zucaro is horrible to everybody."

That seemed to satisfy Donya. But Donya hadn't heard the whole poem. She hadn't heard the line about slimnastics. Unless Mr. Zucaro had told plump girls in his other study halls to do their slim-nastics after school, that line of the poem all but guaranteed that Mr. Zucaro would focus his search on their study hall alone.

That night Bethany took out her problems list and made a new entry:

Problem: Ode to Mr. Zucaro in Springtime
Seriousness: VVVVVS
What to Do: Nothing

What learned? That was a hard one. Not to trust Jane? But Jane was still Bethany's best friend. If Bethany didn't trust Jane, she didn't trust anyone. Not to write poems? That seemed to go too far. Finally Bethany wrote, "Don't write anything about someone else that you wouldn't want them to read." The good thing in her life that made up for this? Bethany picked up her pen and again wrote in her small, neat handwriting, "Nothing."

Bethany's mother and Brooke both came to sit on Bethany's bed as she got dressed Saturday evening for Donya's party. David had to work at the store that night, so Brooke was home for a quiet evening of reading and flute practice. Brandon was outside in the April twilight, kicking a soccer ball back and forth with his father.

"I can fix your hair," Brooke offered.

"Donya said if I came early she'd make French braids for me," Bethany told her.

"Oh, let Brooke do it, honey," Bethany's mother said. "Donya's going to be busy enough fussing over her own hair. And you want to arrive at the party looking as pretty as can be."

Bethany didn't really see why. The only other

guests at the party were going to be the same old sixth-grade girls from her class at school, without Jane and Nicole. Even if Donya's mother had let her invite boys, they would have been the same old sixth-grade boys Bethany saw every day.

Brooke picked up Bethany's comb and brush and stood behind her at her low vanity. "This'll be fun," she said. "I haven't fixed anybody's hair in ages. I haven't even been to a party in ages. Once you have a boyfriend, you don't go to parties much anymore. You'd rather go out just the two of you."

"You'll go to plenty of parties in college," her mother said. "I loved all my college parties, maybe because I didn't go to many parties in high school or junior high. I guess back then I was too academically minded to fit in with the popular crowd, and my family could never afford to buy me the right clothes or shoes. You girls are lucky, to be smart *and* popular. I just hope that you take full advantage of it, that you enjoy it all."

Bethany knew her mother was talking mainly to Brooke: don't get so wrapped up in David that you miss out on all your senior-year parties and activities. But she knew her mother would have said the same thing to her if she had known how close

Bethany had come to refusing to go to Donya's party.

At first it looked as if Donya's party was going to be like all the rest of the popular-girl parties Bethany had attended in the last couple of years. At those parties, the girls wore skinny jeans and fancy tops and as much makeup as their mothers would let them put on. They admired one another's jewelry and exclaimed over one another's hair. After a while, they danced to their favorite CDs and voted on a prize for the best dancer. Sometimes Donya won, sometimes Evie. They had cake and ice cream and diet Coke; then the birthday girl opened presents, and everyone went home.

It didn't seem too tragic to Bethany that Nicole was left out of parties like these. But of course if you were left out, you never had a chance to find out how boring the parties were. Bethany had to admit that she wouldn't have wanted to be the only one uninvited.

And as it turned out, Donya's party *was* different. After she had cut the cake and opened her presents, Donya motioned the girls into a circle around her. "I have an announcement to make," she said. "Do you know how in college they have fraternities and sororities?"

Some girls, including Bethany, didn't.

"They're like clubs, only better than clubs. They're for boys only or girls only, and the boys in a fraternity call each other brothers, and the girls in a sorority call each other sisters. You have to be picked to join, and it's really hard to get in, and once you're in, you can keep out anyone you want. Nobody can get in unless every single member votes for her to join. Then you have a special initiation you have to go through, like all wearing something awful to school on the same day. Oh, and fraternities and sororities are named after Greek letters. Like my father was a member of Sigma Phi Epsilon. And you can get matching T-shirts that say the name of your fraternity or sorority."

Donya paused, and Evie said, "Tell about getting pinned."

"You can also get pins with the name of your fraternity or sorority on them, and if a boy gives his fraternity pin to a girl, then she's pinned, and that's the same as being preengaged, like engaged to be engaged." Donya turned to Evie. "Does a girl ever give her pin to a boy?"

"I don't think so. Maybe sororities don't have pins, just T-shirts. We can find out," Evie said.

"*Anyway,*" Donya said, "Evie and I are starting a sorority, and we've voted on all of you here to be members."

Donya smiled serenely as the questions came thick and fast.

"What's its name?"

"Are we going to have an initiation?"

"Will we get T-shirts?"

"Are the boys going to start a fraternity?"

"All right," Donya said. "The name of our sorority is Delta Eta Delta. That's Greek for D. E. D., which just happen to be the initials of—"

"Douglas Edward Dogan!" someone said. Doug was the best-looking boy in their class, even if Mr. Zucaro thought he grinned too much.

"There's definitely going to be an initiation, but Evie and I haven't decided what it is yet. We checked about the T-shirts, and we can get them printed at T-Shirts and Things, at the mall, for seven dollars each. I don't know if the boys will start a fraternity. But when we all come to school wearing our Delta Eta Delta T-shirts, you can bet they'll notice."

"And it's a secret," Evie added. "You are all sworn to secrecy never to reveal what Delta Eta Delta stands for. Do you promise? Raise your right hands and say, 'I do.' "

Bethany raised her hand with the others. The only person she'd want to tell was Jane, and Jane was sure to guess, anyway.

"Are we members now?" someone asked.

"Not yet. When you become a member, it's called pledging, and you do it after the initiation."

"What about Jane?" someone else asked.

Bethany felt the others looking over at her.

"Is Jane going to be a member?"

"I don't know," Donya said. "It depends on how we vote. But, remember, one 'no' vote and she's out."

"What about Tums?"

General laughter. Bethany didn't join in, but she didn't shout, "Stop laughing!" either.

"We'll vote," Donya said again.

"She's out," Evie said. "I already know how I'm voting, so she's out."

What about Bethany? She didn't want to be in any club that Jane wasn't in. She didn't want to be in any club that Nicole wasn't in. But what would her mother say if she found out that Bethany wasn't a member of Mountainview Elementary School's first sorority? "You girls are lucky, to be smart *and* popular. I just hope that you take full advantage of it, that you enjoy it all." And her mother would find out. Her women's group was meeting next week, and Donya's mother would tell her. There was no way on earth she wouldn't find out.

10

Bethany's father came to pick her up from Donya's party at ten o'clock. "Did you have a good time, honey?" he asked as he backed carefully out of Donya's steep, curved driveway.

"Uh-huh," Bethany answered automatically. What would her father do if she said, "Not really. First of all, I don't even like Donya very much, and second of all, I can't have a good time doing anything when any minute the phone might ring and it might be Mr. Zucaro telling you and Mom that I wrote a satiric poem about him."

Maybe she *should* say it? It might be easier to

talk to her father than to her mother. He was more easygoing; he had a good sense of humor. Bethany's mother said that Bethany's father never could have been an indexer because he didn't *agonize* enough over things.

"Actually," Bethany began, but they were already turning onto Hillside Avenue, Bethany's street. They would be home in another minute.

"Actually?" her father asked.

"No, it *was* fun," Bethany said. "It's just that—"

"You're not really a party girl," her father finished the sentence for her.

It wasn't what Bethany had meant to say, but now her father was reaching for the garage-door opener, and her mother would be waiting to hear about what the other girls had worn to the party and how they had fixed their hair.

"I guess that's it," Bethany said.

"I'm not that big on parties myself," her father said. He gave her shoulder a gentle pat. "And, believe me, they don't get any more thrilling when you're grown-up. I'd say eight's about the cutoff. Brandon has five more good party years, and then, forget it."

Inside, Bethany's mother gave her an absent-minded hug. "Did you have fun, sweetheart?"

Bethany nodded. "Is Brooke around?"

She already knew the answer. Her mother seemed distracted, as if she wasn't really listening to Bethany's reply to her question.

"No. David stopped by after work to pick her up, and they went out for some french fries. She said she'd be home by midnight, although why it takes two hours to eat a plate of french fries I'm sure I don't know."

"Come on, Anne," Bethany's father said. "Quit worrying. They have to dip each fry in ketchup, and after each bite they have to talk for a while, and look out the window at the moon, and predict the winners in every category of the Academy Awards, and that'll keep them hungry enough that when they're done they'll probably order a second plateful of fries, and maybe some onion rings, too. I say let's all go to bed. Brooke has a key. She can let herself in when she gets home."

Bethany went to bed when her parents did, but she couldn't sleep. What if Mr. Zucaro got a book out of the library on handwriting analysis? Even if Jane had made her writing small and messy, it would still look like Jane's writing, only smaller and messier. She would still have formed her letters the same way. What if Doug Dogan, who sat behind Bethany in math, had seen her scribbling away on the poem during the review session?

Mr. Zucaro was going to know that the culprits were Bethany and Jane. He had to find out. When people wanted to find out something badly enough, usually they did. What would Bethany's mother do when he called her? What would she say? Would she start looking at Bethany the way she looked at Brandon, with the same kind of despairing worry in her eyes?

Bethany turned her pillow over, to lay her cheek against the smoother side, and scrunched her eyes shut. She still wasn't sleepy. She flipped over so that she was facing away from the window and pulled the covers up around her chin.

Would Bethany get an A on her Afghanistan report, or only an A-minus because she had taken too much stuff from the *National Geographic*? Her index wasn't such a great thing anymore, now that Mr. Shapiro knew that her mother was an indexer.

What if Jane figured out what Delta Eta Delta

stood for and told Doug and the other boys, and then Donya and Evie thought that Bethany had broken her vow and told Jane?

What would Jane and Nicole say when the other girls all wore their Delta Eta Delta T-shirts to school on the same day? What would Mr. Zucaro say?

The last thought made Bethany smile in the darkness. What *would* he say? "Please hold your fashion shows after school. . . ."

Bethany must have fallen asleep, because when she looked at the clock again, it said 12:45. Bethany knew—she could feel it from the tense quality of the stillness in the house—that Brooke wasn't home. Silently she slipped from bed and tiptoed next door to peek into Brooke's room. Brooke's door was open, her room was dark, her neatly made bed was empty. Downstairs there was a light on in the kitchen. Bethany heard the low singsong of her parents' voices, but she couldn't make out what they were saying.

One o'clock. Still no Brooke.

Bethany wrapped a blanket around her shoulders and went to sit on her window seat, overlooking Hillside Avenue. No one was up in any of the neighbors' houses, unless, like Bethany, someone was curled up in the dark, waiting.

At 1:15, David's car turned in to their driveway. At least Brooke was all right. At least there hadn't been a car accident.

From downstairs Bethany heard Brooke's voice, a little too loud and cheerful. "Sorry I'm late. You didn't need to wait up."

She heard her mother's voice next, quick and angry, then her father's voice, angry, too.

"But I'm almost eighteen!"

Bethany climbed back into bed. She buried her face in her pillow, but she could still hear voices. Someone was crying. Brooke? Or her mother?

Then Brooke's footsteps pounded on the stairs.

"You never liked David. You're snobs, both of you—snobs!"

Brooke's door slammed. This time Bethany could hear that the crying was Brooke's. But downstairs there was crying, too.

Finally the house was quiet. When Bethany was sure her parents were asleep, she turned on the small lamp next to her bed. If she read for a bit, she might begin to feel drowsy. From her bookshelf

Bethany chose a book she had already read three or four times: *On the Banks of Plum Creek*. Maybe if she read about the Ingalls family losing their precious wheat crop to a plague of grasshoppers, her own problems wouldn't seem as big.

A tap on the door startled her.

The door opened, and Brooke poked her head in. "I saw your light."

"I couldn't sleep," Bethany said.

Brooke's eyes were red-rimmed, and she was still clutching a balled-up tissue. She sat down on the edge of Bethany's bed.

"Did you hear them? Yelling at me? Before?"

"Some of it."

Brooke looked at the book in Bethany's hand. "When Laura Ingalls Wilder was my age, she was *married*. And they think it's a big deal if I stay out one hour late. I didn't know you were supposed to have a Ph.D. in nuclear physics before you could have a *boyfriend*."

Bethany closed her book and laid it next to her on the quilt. Brooke had never talked to her like this before, as if the two of them were the same age, and friends. But at one-thirty in the morning there weren't a lot of other people she could talk to.

"They don't like David," Brooke said. "At least Mom doesn't."

Bethany knew Brooke was right, but she said, "Mom said he's a pleasant young man. Or something like that. The other day, when you two were baby-sitting for Brandon."

"I know why, too," Brooke said as if Bethany hadn't spoken. "It's because he's not going to college, and he works in a video store. Like those are really great reasons not to like someone. Sometimes they're such snobs, both of them, it makes me want to scream. It makes me want to never read a book again in my life, and to get all C's, and give my flute away to the Salvation Army."

Brooke picked up *On the Banks of Plum Creek*. "Is this the one with Nellie Oleson? She's the mean girl, right, who makes fun of Laura and Mary for being country girls?"

"Uh-huh. And it's the one with the grasshoppers."

"But it's like—Almanzo Wilder didn't go to college. He was just a farmer. Laura was just a farmer's wife. Why does it matter how much money someone makes? Why isn't it enough just to be happy?"

Bethany didn't know what to say.

"Can you keep a secret?" Brooke asked then.

Bethany nodded, but she had the terrible feeling that she wasn't going to like Brooke's secret, whatever it was.

"I've decided—" Brooke looked down at the book as she spoke, not at Bethany. "I've decided . . . David is *important* to me. You'll have a boyfriend someday, Bethany. Then you'll understand. I know Mom and Dad think this is just an infatuation, but it's not like I'm in junior high school. It's not like I have some kind of infantile crush on a little boy. I've decided . . . I'm not going away to college next year. I'm not going away from David. I'm not."

Bethany felt as if she had been punched in the stomach. "But you *have* to go. You have to go to *college*."

"Not two thousand miles away from David, I don't. I can go to the University of Colorado, right here in state. There's nothing wrong with CU. I mean, I can't go in September because I didn't apply, so I'll have to take a year off, but a lot of people take a year off."

"How are you—you can't keep it a *secret*. Mom

and Dad will notice if September comes and you're still *here*."

All along Bethany had felt herself on Brooke's side. Brooke deserved to have the boyfriend she wanted, even if he wasn't a super student. But now, suddenly, Bethany felt a surge of anger toward Brooke. It was bad enough that Brandon didn't really talk; if Brooke didn't go to college, it would break their mother's heart. There weren't enough long words in the entire unabridged dictionary that Bethany could learn to make up for a disappointment that big. Brooke acted as if being in love with someone meant that you didn't owe anything to anybody else.

You can't do this to Mom, Brooke; you can't do this to *me*.

"Obviously I have to tell them," Brooke said impatiently. "But maybe I won't get accepted anywhere. Maybe it'll all work itself out. Or maybe—anyway, the later I tell them, the better. Maybe I'll turn down all the colleges first, and then I'll tell Mom when it's too late for her to make me change my mind."

Brooke looked so close to tears that Bethany held back her angry words. All she said was, "But what if you turn them all down, and then over the summer you and David . . ."

"Break up? Oh, that would be convenient for Mom and Dad, wouldn't it? Sorry, Bethany. David and I aren't going to break up. I should have known you wouldn't understand, either. I'm going to bed. Good night."

Brooke got up from the bed and walked to the door. Then she came back and hugged Bethany, awkwardly. They weren't the kind of sisters who hugged a lot.

"I'm sorry. You didn't mean anything. It's just— do you think I *want* to let them down? Do you think it makes me feel great to think about what Mom will say after I tell her?"

Bethany hugged Brooke back.

"Good night," Brooke said again. "Thank you, Bethany. I know I can count on you to keep a secret."

11
....

Bethany slept late the next morning, and once awake, she stayed for almost half an hour in bed. She read another chapter in her book. Then she closed her eyes and just lay motionless, listening to the neighbor's lawn mower and to Brandon's whoops as he jumped on the trampoline. She didn't want to see her parents or Brooke. She didn't even want to see Brandon.

But when she finally made herself go downstairs, everything was so peaceful and normal that last night's argument seemed like a scene from the wrong TV show that had shown up on the screen by mistake. Brooke, still in her nightgown, sat eating a yogurt, while her father read the Sunday paper and her mother watered the plants.

"Watch me!" Brandon shouted. Even though Bethany had seen him jump on the trampoline a thousand times, and every time was the same, she stood and watched him and clapped when he was done.

"What do you want for breakfast, sleepyhead?" her father asked.

"Cereal," Bethany said. "I'll get it."

"Last night we didn't have much of a chance to talk about Donya's party," Bethany's mother said. "How was it? Tell me everything—all the details."

"It was just a party," Bethany said.

"Did the other girls like how Brooke fixed your hair?"

"Uh-huh."

"Brooke, you'll have to give me a crash course in beautifying Bethany so that I can carry on when you head east next fall," Bethany's mother said.

Brooke shot a look at Bethany then, a look that told Bethany that she still meant what she had said last night—every word of it.

"Today isn't really April thirteenth, is it?"

Bethany's father asked, glancing at the large calendar that hung on the side of the refrigerator. "I guess I'd better spend this afternoon on the taxes."

"Remember the year you forgot to look at the calendar until the fifteenth was already past?" Bethany's mother asked. "It must have been the year Bethany was in kindergarten—she had so much artwork up on the fridge that it covered the calendar, and when you finally got around to checking it, it was already April eighteenth."

"Seventeenth," her father said. He had heard the story before. The whole family had heard the story before.

"But we're not going to make any mistakes this year," Bethany's mother said. "We all know that April fifteenth is this Tuesday; isn't it, Brooke, honey? It's a big day for everyone. Including Brandon. His three-year-old checkup is this Tuesday, too. Brandon, sweetheart, no shots this time! We're only going to the doctor so she can tell us what a healthy, wonderful boy you are."

Bethany's mother spoke in a light, merry tone, but then she turned abruptly away from the table and began loading the breakfast dishes into the dishwasher. If only Dr. Carter would say that Brandon *was* a healthy, wonderful boy who talked just the right amount for his age.

"Why doesn't the IRS just take all the money up front and then mail back the little bit they decide to let us keep?" Bethany's father asked, pushing his chair back from the table. "It'd be easier on everyone that way."

When Bethany went upstairs to get dressed, she scribbled three new entries on the problems list: Delta Eta Delta, Brooke and college, and Brandon's checkup. For Dr. Carter was sure to say *something* about Brandon's talking. That was just the kind of thing doctors checked at checkups. She might say that Brandon talked the right amount, but what if she said there was something wrong with Brandon for not talking more? What would Bethany's mother do then?

Delta Eta Delta: VVS
Brooke and college: VVS
Brandon's checkup: VVS

Bethany stared at the chart in despair. What good was it to cross Donya's party off the checklist, if three new VVS problems were added in its place?

"A sorority?" Jane burst out laughing when Bethany told her that afternoon in the tree fort.

"I guess I'm in it," Bethany said. "But . . . when they vote on you, I don't know if Evie . . . And Donya's pretty mad that you didn't go to her party."

"Like I care," Jane said. "Like I would be in their sorority if they paid me. What's its name again?"

"Delta Eta Delta."

"How did they come up with that?"

"It's—they made us promise we wouldn't tell."

"Oh, by all means, let us keep our promises," Jane said. "Delta Eta Delta. D. E. D.? Okay, I get it. It's Douggy-Wuggy Eddy-Weddy-Beddy Dogan, isn't it? No, don't tell! You must be true to your sisters and not betray their secrets to evil outsiders."

Bethany couldn't tell if Jane sounded hurt. Sometimes with Jane it was hard to know.

"They're not my sisters. And, yes, you're right. That's what it stands for."

If Bethany had to be in a club that excluded Jane, at least she could break its rules for Jane, and she and Jane could laugh at it together. And if Nicole wanted to know the secret behind Delta Eta Delta's name, Bethany would tell her, too.

On Monday, Bethany was heading outside with her gym class for softball when Ms. Kohler tapped her on the shoulder. The gym teacher had a note in her hand.

"Bethany, you're wanted in the office."

"In the office?"

Bethany had never been summoned to the office. She stood still, hardly knowing what to do.

"Yes, in Mr. Ryan's office. So run along. I'll assign you to a team when you get back."

Bethany had no choice but to go. She knew the summons had to be about Mr. Zucaro. It had to be. She walked down the long, empty corridor from the gym to the central office as if she were a condemned prisoner marching at dawn to her execution.

When she reached the office, Bethany stood uncertainly in the front work area, where the three school secretaries had their desks.

"May I help you?" one of the secretaries asked.

"Ms. Kohler said . . . I was wanted in the office."

The secretary consulted a list of names on her desk. "Are you Bethany Barrett? Go on in. Mr. Ryan's office is the first door to the left."

"Bethany? Come in! Sit down!"

Mr. Ryan called to her as if they were old friends, but in fact the only time they had ever spoken was the day that Bethany had run back to get her poem and found him guarding the school's main entrance. His pleasant tone somehow seemed more terrifying than a stern one would have been.

"I'm sorry to take you away from class," Mr. Ryan said. "But Mr. Zucaro has been having problems maintaining an orderly, quiet atmosphere in the library, and he asked me to speak to several students whom he considers central to his efforts to make the library an inviting place to study."

Bethany sat tense and straight in the chair Mr. Ryan had shown her, gripping the edge of her seat tightly with both hands.

"I know you're a good student, Bethany, so you must understand how important it is to have a quiet time and place to study. I'm sure I can count on you to help make our study halls just that: *study halls*."

"Okay," Bethany made herself say. Was that all? It couldn't be.

"Oh, and one more thing, Bethany." Mr. Ryan said it as if it were an afterthought. "Some student—we believe it was a student in your study hall—recently wrote a poem about Mr. Zucaro that upset him a great deal. Do you know anything about this poem?"

Bethany shook her head. She didn't trust her voice. If there were a lie detector anywhere in the state of Colorado, she knew that by now it must be setting off flashing lights and blaring sirens.

Mr. Ryan looked almost embarrassed then, but he went on: "Ms. Kanowith, your English teacher, mentioned that you wrote some fine poems for her class last fall."

Bethany hardly breathed.

"But you don't know anything about the poem Mr. Zucaro is talking about." Mr. Ryan made it a statement, not a question, but it felt like a question.

"Okay, Bethany, here's a pass to send you back to class. Would you tell Ms. Kohler that I'd like to speak next to Jane Owen? Thank you. Hit a home run for me!"

Once she was in the main corridor again, Bethany's knees began to tremble violently. Was Mr. Ryan questioning everyone in their class? Or only those students—how had Mr. Ryan put it?—central to the effort to make the library an inviting place to study? In a word: *suspects*. She was one, and Jane was another. How many more were there?

Bethany had no chance to warn Jane, or to speak to Jane after she returned to class. Donya went to the office after Jane, and Evie after Donya. Was Mr. Ryan also going to summon Nicole?

When gym class was finally over, Bethany and Jane walked together to lunch.

"I didn't crack!" Jane said. "Even when Mr. Ryan said, 'Mr. Zucaro believes that your handwriting is somewhat similar to the handwriting in the poem.'"

"I didn't crack, either," Bethany said. "Even when he said that Ms. Kanowith said I write good poems."

"I can't believe they're going to so much trouble about a poem," Jane said. "I mean, a poem is only words. It's like, sticks and stones can break your bones, but words can never hurt you."

"Well, but . . . in a way, words hurt more than sticks and stones," Bethany said slowly. "Calling Nicole Tums. That hurts more than just pulling her hair, or something. And learning all our genius words—we wouldn't do it if we didn't think that words *mattered*."

"You're right," Jane said. "But I don't know. Didn't you kind of get the feeling that Mr. Ryan was—well, that he didn't really want to be asking us those questions, but that Mr. Zucaro was making him do it?"

"I know what you mean. But if they find out it was us, what do you think they'll do?"

"I don't know." Jane sounded less brave than usual. "Burn us at the stake, I guess."

After school Donya and Evie lingered at the bike racks with Jane and Bethany to compare notes, huddling together against the wind.

"He talked to you two, and me and Donya, and Tums, and four of the boys," Evie said. "That makes nine suspects, total."

"He told me that Mr. Zucaro said I laugh too much in study hall," Donya said. "Laugh too much!"

"He said he had heard I wrote good poems!" Bethany said, to join in the conversation and make clear that she, too, thought the whole search was ridiculous.

"You do write good poems," Donya said. She looked at Bethany a bit strangely then.

"So do lots of people," Jane said. "Hey, maybe a ghost wrote the poem. Maybe it was the ghost of Henry Wadsworth Longfellow. 'Listen, my children, and you shall hear / Of the librarian we hate and fear.' "

"*I* don't," Evie said. "I don't write good poems, and neither does Donya. But all I know is, whoever wrote this poem is in big, big trouble."

12
. . . . .

The mail truck was pulling away from the mail-box just as Bethany turned onto Hillside Avenue on her way home from school. A whole minute went by without Brooke's racing out of the house, so Brooke must not be home, or else Brooke had decided she didn't care about the mail anymore.

Bethany opened the box and took out the day's stack of mail: two magazines, a grocery-store cir-cular, a bill from Public Service, a letter for her mother from a publishing company, and a letter for Brooke from Yale University.

A *thick* letter for Brooke from Yale University.

Even though it was only April fourteenth, there it was. As fat as could be, it had to be an acceptance letter—Brooke's first, and from her first-choice university, too.

Bethany sandwiched the letter into the pile, between the grocery circular and the magazines. She went inside and set the pile on the front-hall table.

Brandon came running to greet her. "Brandon made peepee!" he shouted.

Bethany hardly listened. As far as she was concerned, Brandon made far too much peepee and far too many poops.

"Brandon made peepee *in the potty!*"

"Brandon!" Bethany fell on her knees and hugged him. That *was* big news. Plus he had just said a six-word sentence. Six words was pretty long for a sentence.

"He really did," Bethany's mother said, coming down the stairs. She looked weary, but triumphant. "I was bound and determined that he make at least one drop of peepee in the potty before we go to see Dr. Carter tomorrow. So this afternoon I coaxed him onto the potty, and nothing happened, and we sat there some more, and nothing happened, and then I gave him a box of juice to drink, and nothing happened, and then he started on his second box—and then: peepee!"

"Peepee in the potty!" Brandon shouted.

"I know Dr. Carter will ask about it. At the three-year checkup they want to hear about some progress in toilet training. And I think that's the checkup where they make a big fuss about hopping on one foot. Tina Gordon said her pediatrician was very concerned back in February when Tavi wasn't hopping. We tried hopping this afternoon, too." Bethany's mother lowered her voice. "He's not ready yet—it was pretty hopeless. But then—oh, Brandon, wait till we tell Daddy and Brooke about your peepee!"

Bethany's mother's glance fell on the hall table. "The mail came? Anything good?"

"I didn't really look at it," Bethany said. "I think you got something from one of your publishers."

"Yes, here it is. It's too soon to be the check for *Europe in*—Yale! Bethany, look: Brooke got a letter from Yale! Oh, I wish she were here to open it, but of course she's out with David. It has to be an acceptance—but I promised her I wouldn't open a thing."

Bethany's mother cleared away the rest of the

mail and propped Brooke's letter against the vase of flowers on the hall table.

"There! She'll see it the moment she walks in. Bethany, could you straighten up in the family room a little bit? Tavi and his mom are coming over to play for an hour before dinner, and Brandon and I have been so busy with *peepee*—and now *Yale!*"

Bethany hurried into the family room and began picking up plastic snap-together blocks and various facial features for Mr. Potato Head. Maybe she should have hidden Brooke's letter before her mother could see it. She should have slipped it into her backpack and left it for Brooke upstairs in her bedroom. But it was too late now.

The doorbell rang.

"Can you get that, honey?" Bethany's mother called from the bathroom.

Bethany opened the front door for Ms. Gordon, Tavi, and Tavi's purple Barry Bear. "Come on in," she said. "Brandon and my mother'll be down in a minute."

If Ms. Gordon saw Brooke's letter from Yale in its place of honor on the hall table, she didn't say anything. But Tavi had plenty to say.

"I learned a new song today, Bethany. It was on

the Barry Bear show, and it has three verses, and I know all three verses, and you clap your hands in a funny way with them, and I can do all the clapping, too."

Bethany didn't count the words in that sentence, but she knew there were more than six. Lots more than six.

Her mother came in with Brandon then.

"Brandon, sweetheart, tell Ms. Gordon your big news!" she said.

Brandon didn't say anything.

"Tell her what you did this afternoon."

Brandon looked down. Bethany wished her mother wouldn't ask him questions like that. It should have been obvious to her by now that Brandon either couldn't or wouldn't answer questions in front of other people, and when he didn't answer it made him look so shy and—Bethany didn't let herself even think the word.

"Tell her what you made in the *potty* this afternoon."

"Peepee," Brandon whispered.

"Peepee!" Ms. Gordon said. "Oh, my! What a *big* boy."

"So excuse the mess," Bethany's mother said.

"We're worn out from all the excitement. And the mail just came, and Brooke got accepted at Yale. We haven't opened the letter yet because she isn't home, but you know how the acceptance letters are always the thick ones."

"You'll have to give her my congratulations," Ms. Gordon said. Something in her tone suggested that she herself had had experience with plenty of thick letters that had turned out in the end to be rejections, so that, personally, she wasn't going to be excited for Brooke until she saw her board the plane for New Haven, Connecticut, in September.

Of course, Brooke *wasn't* going to be boarding the plane for New Haven in September, unless she changed her mind about David. Bethany could imagine what Ms. Gordon would think come September, when Brooke was still in Pinevale. What a shame about Brooke, but you know how sometimes when you aim *too* high, you miss out completely. . . .

"Tavi learned a new song today," Ms. Gordon said. "Do you want to sing it for us, Tavi?"

"It has three verses," Tavi said. "I know them all, and I can do the clapping, too. Watch me! Oh, Barry Bear's a friend of mine. Barry is my friend. I have fun with Barry Bear. Our fun will never end! That's the first verse. Barry likes to sing with me. Barry likes to play. Barry Bear gives lots of hugs. We sing and play all day! That's the second verse. Oh, Barry likes the sun and rain. He likes the rain and sun. Barry can be your friend, too. He's friends with everyone! That's the end!"

Tavi's mother clapped, so Bethany's mother clapped, too.

"I know two more Barry Bear songs," Tavi said.

"Why don't you go sing them for Brandon?" Bethany's mother said quickly. "I bet he'd love it if you two went to his room and sang them there."

"Okay, Brandon, let's go!" Tavi shouted.

The two boys raced off to Brandon's room.

"Brandon must have had his three-year-old checkup already," Ms. Gordon said when they heard Brandon's door slam shut.

"Tomorrow," Bethany's mother said. "In fact, we made the peepee today just in Dr. Carter's honor." She laughed.

Ms. Gordon smiled, but then she said, "I think at three it's mainly going to be language development that your pediatrician will be concerned about."

Bethany couldn't stand it anymore. "I'd better go practice my violin," she said.

On her way upstairs, she heard her mother changing the subject back to Brooke and Yale. "I guess we'll have to rustle up some kind of celebration for her tonight. It's a pretty big milestone, your first college acceptance letter. . . ."

Ms. Gordon and Tavi left before Brooke came home to open her letter. So Ms. Gordon didn't get to see that, yes, it *was* an acceptance letter, and not the world's first thick rejection.

Brooke shrieked when she began reading it. "I can't believe it! I got in! To Yale!"

She threw herself into her father's arms for a hug. If Bethany had thought Brooke would be upset by her letter, she was wrong.

"Maybe you'll hear from Radcliffe or Princeton tomorrow," her mother said. "But if you got into Yale, I'm sure you'll get in everywhere."

"Yale's the best," Brooke said. "For me, at least. They have the best theater department, if I want to study theater, and the best French department, if I decide to major in French. I only applied to all the others in case I didn't get into Yale. I knew from the very beginning that I wanted to go there."

"It still wouldn't be a bad idea to check out all your options," Bethany's father said. "Why don't you and Mom take a long weekend and fly back East? I have enough frequent-flier miles to cover the tickets, and at this point it won't hurt to miss a couple of days of school. You can make a more informed decision if you actually see these places, walk around the campuses, check out which have the best-looking guys. . . ."

Brooke's face changed. All at once the joy drained out of it.

"Just kidding," her father said quickly. "I mean, check out which have the best-equipped physics labs! Anyway, tonight we celebrate. Brooke picks the place: Mexican, Thai—or how about that new place up on Thomas Mountain that's supposed to have such great views?"

Brooke shook her head almost fiercely. "I can't go out to dinner. Not tonight. I have a test tomorrow in French."

"I'm sure you'll get an A, honey," her mother said. "Just this once, you can—"

"I have to *study*," Brooke said. "In fact, I'd better go upstairs and start right now."

"This weekend, then!" her father called after her. He turned to look at her mother in bewilderment.

"She'd forget about studying fast enough if David knocked at the door," Bethany's mother said.

"Oh, well, she's bound to have mixed emotions about going away in the fall," her father said.

"Mixed emotions about getting into *Yale*?"

"First love feels pretty special," he said.

"We'd better call out for pizza, I guess," Bethany's mother said. "I certainly don't have anything ready for dinner, what with Brandon's peepee—oh, honey, tell Daddy about your peepee!"

Bethany couldn't sleep again that night. She read *On the Banks of Plum Creek* all the way to the end, but she still couldn't sleep. Okay, having a plague of grasshoppers destroy your family's whole wheat crop would be worse than having a sister who didn't want to go away to college. But having a brother who was slow in talking was worse than losing one year's harvest of wheat. You could plant the wheat again next year, but Bethany couldn't shake the memory of her mother's lie about Brandon's age at King Soopers. If only her mother didn't take things so hard. What would her mother do tomorrow if Dr. Carter said there was something seriously wrong with Brandon? Maybe Bethany could call Dr. Carter and warn her: "My brother doesn't talk as much as he's supposed to, but don't tell my mom!"

Even Bethany could see how ridiculous that was.

As far as phone calls went, she would be lucky if her mother didn't get a phone call of her own from Mr. Zucaro tomorrow. Was it worse to be caught by Mr. Zucaro or to face a plague of grasshoppers? Mr. Zucaro was actually fairly similar to a plague of grasshoppers, in the way he kept on marching forward toward his goal, devouring everything in his path.

Bethany slipped out of bed to stare at her problems list one last time.

Zipper on blue jeans—NS
Brandon's talking—VVS
Ode to Mr. Zucaro in Springtime—VVVVVS
Delta Eta Delta—VVS

Brooke and college—VVS
Brandon's checkup—VVS

Maybe Bethany would tell her mother about the zipper on the blue jeans tomorrow, after Brandon's checkup. That would be at least one problem crossed off the list. And Brandon's checkup would be crossed off the list then, too, for better or worse.

Maybe Bethany should just hand the whole list to her mother: "Here. Here is everything I don't want you to know about." That would solve most of the problems on the list, too. After all, the whole point of the problems list was just to keep her mother from finding out too much: about the torn zipper, about Mr. Zucaro, about Brooke, about Brandon—about Bethany.

What would happen if Bethany did that? Just sat down and told her mother every problem on her list? Telling her could hardly be worse than not telling her was turning out to be. But how would she do it? Where would she begin? And when she was finished, what would her mother say?

Bethany couldn't do it. She didn't . . . know how.

She climbed back into bed and tucked her problems list under her pillow. If only the tooth fairy would come in the night to take it away! But she had learned long ago that the tooth fairy was really her mother.

13
.....

*T*he next morning David came to the house early, before breakfast, to give Brooke a ride to school. Brooke must have called him the night before with her news, because when Bethany answered the door he was holding a single daffodil in his hand.

"For Miss Ivy League," he told Bethany.

Bethany wanted to ask him if he would still like Brooke if she went away to college. Maybe if he and Brooke were really serious, he could move to New Haven with her and find a job in a video store there. Every town had a video store. That would make more sense than Brooke's giving up her college dreams to stay in Colorado. Bethany wanted Brooke to go away to college so much that she could hardly bear it, not only for her mother's sake, but for Brooke's sake, too. But she didn't want Brooke to have to give up David, either.

All Bethany said was, "She'll be right down."

She knew it was wrong to spy, but she couldn't help lingering for a little while in the front hallway, rearranging her books in her backpack, as she waited for Brooke to appear.

Finally Brooke came down the stairs to the living room.

"For my smart girl," David said, holding out the flower.

"But, David—"

Bethany couldn't hear the rest of what Brooke whispered to him, but she could hear the pain in Brooke's voice.

"Just take it," David told her gently. "It's all going to work out. We'll make it work out. Pretend like it's a movie, and we can make it end however we want it to. I mean, if God had wanted everybody in the world to stay in Pinevale, he wouldn't have invented airplanes, and telephones, and the U.S. Postal Service."

Brooke let David tuck the daffodil into her hair. Then they went out to David's car. Bethany didn't know how David was going to make things work out, but she had a feeling that anyone who had been so smart at outwitting Mr. Teets wasn't going to be dumb enough to let someone he loved give up her dreams.

At Bethany's school that morning, no one was called for any further interviews with Mr. Ryan. Still, every time she heard footsteps in the hallway, Bethany tensed in her seat, expecting the door to burst open with a second summons to the office.

In social studies, Mr. Shapiro handed back the country reports. Bethany got an A on her report on Afghanistan. At the top of her index, Mr. Shapiro had written, "Even an index! Wow!" But one A in social studies wouldn't make it up to her mother for the disgrace of being expelled or suspended from school once Mr. Zucaro finally discovered her identity.

Brandon's doctor's appointment was at 11:30, while Bethany had gym class. So all during gym, Bethany's heart clenched like a hard fist inside her. At that very moment Dr. Carter would be delivering her verdict. At that very moment, Bethany's mother would be listening to whatever Dr. Carter had to say. And at that moment more college acceptance letters were probably speeding in the mail truck toward the Barretts' wood-shingled mailbox on Hillside Avenue.

In study hall, Mr. Zucaro waited until everyone was seated. Then he cleared his throat. "You may remember the incident last week in which a certain poem was circulated, a poem that mocked my efforts to keep order in this library."

The silence in the library was vast and endless, like the silence of deep space out beyond the farthest galaxy.

"Mr. Ryan and I have made some inquiries, and we believe we have now identified the author of this unfortunate piece of *literature*."

Silence, like the silence of the ages before the universe began.

"Would this person please be so kind as to step down the hall to explain her poetic undertakings to Mr. Ryan?"

Her poetic undertakings.

"I am talking to *you*," Mr. Zucaro said, looking directly at Bethany's table. "To you, Miss Jane Owen."

The silence in the room focused, laserlike, on

Jane. Without a word, looking at no one, Jane collected her books. Then she walked out of the room and shut the door behind her.

No one so much as whispered. For once, Doug Dogan wasn't smiling. Nicole looked close to tears. Donya and Evie exchanged a glance. Bethany saw it. She thought, They're glad. They're glad it was Jane.

What would they do to her? *Could* you be expelled for writing a poem? Somehow Bethany felt as if Jane were being sent off to be executed, but of course she wasn't. They couldn't burn a sixth grader at the stake for writing a funny poem about a teacher. But Bethany also couldn't believe that a criminal pursued at such length could receive an ordinary, everyday punishment. Certainly at the very least they would call Jane's parents.

Would Jane talk? Bethany knew she wouldn't. Jane would sit stubbornly silent and never betray Bethany. Bethany *could* trust Jane. Of all the problems on her problems list, "Ode to Mr. Zucaro in Springtime" was rated the most serious. Now she would be able to cross it off the list forever. Jane would be the one in trouble, not Bethany. Bethany's mother would never need to know about it, any more than she would need to know about Bethany's friendship with Jane.

But Jane had looked even skinnier than usual as she walked out of the library. Although her face hadn't shown any emotion, there had been something about her back, the slope of her narrow shoulders, that had made her look small and scared.

"I trust you will employ the next twenty-five minutes profitably, in silent study," Mr. Zucaro said to the class. "And now, if you will excuse me for the rest of the period, Miss Allen, my aid, will supervise you while I join Miss Owen in conference with Mr. Ryan."

Right now Jane was probably sitting down in Mr. Ryan's office. Even if they tortured her, Jane wouldn't tell. Bethany's secret was safe with Jane. Bethany was free.

Mr. Zucaro, briefcase in hand, was heading out the library door.

Bethany's own silence swelled in her throat, choking her, cutting off her breath. Her thoughts were all confused, but it suddenly seemed to her as if she would never be free if she let Jane go all alone to her doom. It seemed that if she didn't speak now she would never speak, and she would spend the rest of her life trapped inside the prison of her own problems list.

"Wait!"

It was her own voice, startling her, as sharp as the explosion of the last GOOD LUCK balloon. Bethany stood up.

"Yes, Miss Barrett? Is there some problem?" Mr. Zucaro turned toward her.

"Jane didn't write that poem."

Mr. Zucaro stood with his hand on the doorknob. "I did."

The silence in the room seemed to recede, so that Bethany could hear Donya's intake of breath, and Nicole's dropped pencil.

"Indeed, Miss Barrett. Why don't you accompany me to the office. I believe Mr. Ryan will be very interested in hearing what you have to say for yourself."

Like Jane before her, Bethany stuffed her books into her backpack. Then she followed Mr. Zucaro out the door.

At least the office was next to the library. If Bethany had had to walk down a full corridor with Mr. Zucaro by her side, she couldn't have done it. But right now she felt something more than terror, more than dread: a kind of wild, reckless exhilaration.

A moment later, she was being ushered into Mr. Ryan's office.

"Bethany!" Jane's voice came in a joyful cry.

Bethany looked at Jane, looked what she could not say, and the sudden gladness in Jane's eyes gave her a jolt of electrifying courage.

"Sit down, girls," Mr. Ryan said in his same pleasant way. "Suppose you tell us the truth now. After talking to both of you yesterday, and to some of your other classmates, Mr. Zucaro and I decided that the evidence against Jane was too strong. The similarities in the handwriting are quite striking, if you overlook some superficial differences. And, Jane, I wish I didn't have to say this, but we have had trouble with you in the past. Last year, for example, when I believe you launched a protest against a Thanksgiving play."

"Columbus Day," Jane said.

"That's right. Ms. Williams made a note for your record to the effect that you were—"

"Antagonistic?"

Mr. Ryan looked surprised. "That's right. That's just the word she used."

"This poem here," Mr. Zucaro said, producing his copy of it from his briefcase, "is certainly antagonistic in tone. But Miss Barrett *now* says that in fact she boasts the distinction of being its author."

The hatred in Mr. Zucaro's voice frightened Bethany. In her whole life, no one had ever really hated her the way Mr. Zucaro did now.

The principal looked at her.

She didn't know if she could make her voice come out. "I wrote it," she finally said in a whisper.

"But I copied it over and put it on the bulletin board," Jane burst out. "Bethany didn't know I did it. She never would have stuck it up there like that. She was mad at me when she found out about it. So it was mostly my fault. I'm the one you should punish, not her."

"But I'm the one who wrote it," Bethany said. This time her voice was stronger.

"Yes, but—there's nothing wrong with *writing* a poem," Jane said. "People have a right to write poems. This is a free country. Writing a poem is part of freedom of speech. But I shouldn't have put it on the bulletin board. I'm . . . sorry I did. Don't punish Bethany; punish me."

"I think you girls can leave decisions about disciplinary action to me," Mr. Ryan said. "Mr. Zucaro, is there anything you would like to say to Jane and Bethany?"

Mr. Zucaro took off his glasses, wiped the lenses with his pocket handkerchief, and put them back on again. He seemed almost at a loss for words.

"I suppose you two think it's easy," he finally said. "I suppose you think it's easy to run four study halls every day, one after the other, and keep one hundred twenty students quiet and well behaved. Talking. Laughing. Whispering. Chewing *gum*. Passing notes back and forth. Pranks. Jokes. Do you think it's pleasant for me, trying to maintain a semblance of order? Is it so comical that a study hall should be a place for young scholars to study?"

Bethany knew that she was supposed to say something. "No," she said. "But . . . I know we're noisy sometimes, but I think . . . it's easier to study with noise than with . . . when people yell at you all the time, *that's* what makes it hard to study. And in the poem, I didn't say anything that wasn't *true*."

Mr. Zucaro picked up the poem again. " 'How dare you think in study hall?' Have I ever forbidden you to think in study hall?"

149

"No, but . . ." Bethany looked at Jane for help. But then she decided: It was *her* poem. She was the one who had to defend it.

"You *did* yell at Doug Dogan for smiling," she said. "And you *did* read Donya's note to Jane out loud to the class. And you *did* tell Nicole to do her slimnastics after school, when you can see she's fat and feels terrible if people tease her about it."

"Nicole? Miss McCloskey? But—oh, come now, all you girls do slimnastics and aerobics and whatever else you call it. I certainly didn't mean—" Mr. Zucaro's voice broke off.

"And you *don't* like us to touch the books," Jane added. "You *don't*."

Mr. Zucaro sighed. "If you could only *see* what the library looks like by the end of eighth period. Books left open, facedown, cracking the spine; books with pages torn, dog-eared; *gum* underneath the bookshelves; litter on the floor . . . But when a student has a legitimate research need, I have always been more than happy to cooperate."

Bethany knew that wasn't true. But she didn't say anything. She had already said enough.

They all sat silently for a moment, and then Mr. Ryan spoke again. "All right, girls, I think you've made your points to Mr. Zucaro, and in a more fair way, I must say, than by posting them in an unsigned poem. And perhaps he'll consider them in setting library policy in the future. Suppose we agree to let bygones be bygones. Jane has apologized for her part in this, and I think Bethany is sorry, too. Isn't that right, Bethany? She never meant for her poem to reach such a wide audience. Does that seem fair enough, Mr. Zucaro?"

Bethany hardly dared look at Mr. Zucaro. After his passionate hunt for the guilty parties, to have it end like this, with no punishment for Jane and Bethany, none at all. . . . She stole one quick glance at him. He sat red-faced—with anger? With embarrassment? Did he still hate her? Did he abhor her the way she abhorred him?

"Here's a pass to your next class," Mr. Ryan said.

A moment later Bethany and Jane stood in the hall—not burned at the stake, not banished for life, not expelled or suspended, not even assigned to two afternoons of detention. Bethany hugged Jane then, and Jane hugged Bethany. One VVVVVS problem: solved!

14

When Bethany and Jane walked together into their next class, the room fell silent with awestruck amazement, as if they had risen from the dead.

"What happened?" Donya called to Bethany in a loud whisper.

"Nothing." It was the shortest version of the truth that Bethany could give before math class began. But when Ms. Harper turned around to the chalkboard to write their problems for the period, Bethany flashed a quick thumbs-up sign to Nicole.

After math, on the way to art, the others crowded around Bethany and Jane.

"Are you going to be suspended?" Doug asked, grinning.

"Are you kicked out of the library, like forever?" Evie asked.

"What did Mr. Zucaro *say*?" Donya asked.

Bethany and Jane looked at each other. It was only fair to tell the others *something*.

"He just said how hard it is making us be quiet and keeping the books from getting messy," Jane said. "Oh, and he hates chewing gum. That's like his most hated thing. And a study hall should be a place for young scholars to study. That's all, really."

"But what are they going to *do*?" Donya asked. "Now that they know it was you?"

"Nothing," Bethany repeated. "Mr. Ryan just gave us a pass back to class. I think he thought Mr. Zucaro kind of overreacted to the whole thing."

"Aw," Doug said. "I thought you'd at least get the electric chair, or something exciting."

"Sorry," Jane said. "Maybe next time."

"Oh, Bethany," Donya said as the others took their seats in the art room. "I almost forgot. There's a Delta Eta Delta meeting after school today at my house. Evie and I are going to announce what the initiation is going to be, and we're going to vote on Jane and Tums."

Bethany's heart sank. Knowing she could cross off the biggest, most horrible problem on her problems list had almost made her forget that all the other problems still remained. Maybe you could never cross off all the problems on a problems list. Maybe life was about facing each problem on the list, one at a time.

Or maybe . . .

Maybe *every* problem wasn't as hard to cross off as Bethany had thought. If she could cross off "Ode to Mr. Zucaro in Springtime," surely there were other problems she could cross off, too. There was only one way to find out.

"Um, Donya?" Bethany said. "I've been thinking about it, and I don't think—I mean, it sounds like a really fun club and all—but I think if everybody isn't going to be in it, like Jane and Nicole, then . . . I don't want to be in it, either."

"Girls!" the art teacher said. "Please be seated. We have a a very exciting project to start on today."

Bethany sat down. Donya sat behind her, so Bethany couldn't see her face. Maybe Donya wouldn't want to be friends anymore. But Donya

154

still acted friendly enough toward Jane, even though Jane hadn't gone to her party. And if Donya told her mother, and her mother told Bethany's mother . . . well, then Bethany would just explain to her mother that she didn't want to be in a club that left some people out. She could tell her mother about Nicole without telling her about Jane. And maybe—today anything seemed possible—maybe someday she could even tell her about Jane.

Bethany hurried home from school, but when she reached her house she stood on the porch for a long moment before pushing open the front door. She wanted to hear about Brandon's checkup, and she didn't want to hear about Brandon's checkup. She wanted to hear that Dr. Carter had said Brandon was every bit as smart as Tavi, even if he didn't talk as much as Tavi did. She didn't want to hear that Dr. Carter had said Ms. Gordon was right about Brandon.

Brandon came running to meet her. He showed Bethany a shiny, round panda-bear sticker, somewhat crumpled from being clutched in his sticky hand.

"Did Dr. Carter give that to you?" Bethany asked.

Brandon nodded. "I have a sticker!" he said.

I have a sticker. It was a perfect four-word sentence: It had a pronoun, and it was in the correct tense, and it had a new word in it, too.

"It's a wonderful sticker," Bethany said over the sudden lump in her throat.

Her mother came downstairs. She looked more or less the same as she always looked. Actually, her eyes were a bit moist, as if she might have been crying, but the worry lines in her forehead weren't quite as deep.

"How was Brandon's checkup?" Bethany asked casually.

"It was ... well, we probably could have skipped the peepee. Dr. Carter didn't seem to be in any great rush about toilet training. She did ask Brandon to hop, and of course he couldn't do it, but apparently the really important motor milestone is being able to pedal a tricycle, and Brandon's been pedaling his since last fall."

Bethany didn't know if she should ask the next question, but she couldn't not ask it.

"What about ... did she think Brandon talks

enough?" Surely Dr. Carter had said *something* about Brandon's language development.

"She said—" Bethany's mother stared down at her hands. "Well, she said that by three most children are fairly verbal, more so than Brandon, but that there are certainly many children who aren't. And of course Brandon is very shy. It isn't as if—I think I was hoping she would be able to tell me— but it's not as if they *know*. It's not as if anyone *knows*. She pretty much said we have to wait and see. And that's probably the hardest thing. But it's—I guess that's all a parent can *ever* do."

"But did Dr. Carter seem *worried*? Did she say there was anything we should do?"

"She gave me the name of a speech therapist who's very good with young children. I just finished talking to her. But you know Dr. Carter. She never seems worried. She knew that I had been worrying, though—how could I help but worry? But basically all she said was that there aren't any guarantees, in medicine or in parenting. Some late talkers are highly intelligent. Whether Brandon's one of them, we just don't know. And it's funny, but even though Dr. Carter didn't say anything to make me feel better, I do feel better. At least, even if we don't know, we know that in a way it's all right not to know."

Bethany's mother wiped her eyes. Then suddenly she looked at Bethany sharply, as if she was really *seeing* Bethany, not just listening to her absentmindedly as she worried about Brandon or Brooke.

"Bethany, *you* haven't been worrying about Brandon, have you?"

Who, me? Worry?

"A little bit. I mean, you know how much Tavi talks, and last week when I was at Tavi's house, Ms. Gordon said—"

"Tina Gordon means well," Bethany's mother said, "but she's a bit too—"

"Captious and carping," Bethany suggested.

"I would have said nosy and opinionated, but you're certainly developing a wonderful vocabulary, Bethany. But, honey, *you* shouldn't be worrying about Brandon. It's my job to worry about Brandon, because I'm his mother—and if worrying were all there was to motherhood, believe me, I'd get the prize for mother of the year. But it's not *your* job to worry about Brandon. You have a big enough job just worrying about Bethany."

Bethany couldn't contradict her there.

She followed her mother into the kitchen and dropped down onto a kitchen chair, weak with the sudden giddiness of relief. Brandon climbed up onto her lap.

"So, speaking of Bethany, how was school today?" her mother asked, as she rinsed the lunch dishes at the sink.

"I got an A on my Afghanistan report," Bethany said.

"Good for you!"

"Mr. Shapiro liked my index."

"And why shouldn't he? A good index is a jewel beyond price!" Bethany's mother said, laughing. "Did anything else exciting happen?"

No, I just turned down membership in Donya's sorority and survived a confrontation with Mr. Zucaro.

No, I just narrowly escaped being suspended, that's all.

"Actually," Bethany said.

"Actually?" Her mother turned to look at her.

"Well, it's kind of a long story."

"Story?" Brandon asked hopefully, bouncing on Bethany's knees.

"Does it have a happy ending?" Bethany's mother asked.

"I think so. But it's, like, a *very* long story."

"We're not going anywhere," Bethany's mother said, settling herself into the chair facing Bethany. "Are we, Brandon?"

Bethany took a deep breath. "Do you remember Jane Owen?"

"Jane Owen?"

"The girl who colored on the zoo wallpaper?"

"Oh, no!" Bethany's mother said. "Is she in this story?"

Bethany nodded. "Jane's in it, and Donya, and Evie, and this girl at school named Nicole, and the mean librarian who took Ms. Levitt's place back in February."

Brooke was in it, too, in a way, and David, but Brooke's part of the story wasn't Bethany's to tell. Brooke would tell her story when she was as ready to tell it as Bethany was ready to tell hers.

"So, anyway, we have this new librarian at school, and his name is Mr. Zucaro, and he's very, very mean, and one day . . ."

Bethany told the whole story: about "Ode to Mr. Zucaro in Springtime"; and Nicole and slimnastics and Tums; and Delta Eta Delta; and the handwriting samples; and the interviews in Mr. Ryan's office; and the grand finale, in which she and Jane didn't get into trouble, after all.

When she was finished, she made herself look at her mother. She couldn't tell if her mother was trying not to laugh, or trying not to cry.

Her mother blew her nose on a tissue. "Yes, I guess I would say that counts as something exciting happening. I don't blame you for not wanting to be in Donya's little club. It really sounds quite cruel to exclude Nicole that way. But I didn't realize that Jane Owen was still around. Somehow I got the idea that her family had moved away."

"She's still around."

"So I see," Bethany's mother said, frowning. "She's still around and still causing trouble."

"Not really," Bethany said. "Or—maybe she causes trouble, but—I think you'd like Jane if you knew her. I like her. I like her a lot."

Bethany's mother looked worried then—but just ordinary worried, not end-of-the-world worried.

"While we're on the subject, I suppose I should ask: are there any other catastrophes in your life that I don't know about?"

Bethany thought for a minute. "I have a torn zipper on my jeans," she said.

"How did that happen?" Her mother sounded irritated. "When did it tear?"

"It just tore," Bethany said. "Like maybe three weeks ago."

"And you're telling me about it now? Really, I don't know why everyone expects mothers to be mind readers. Bring the jeans downstairs, and I'll mend the zipper this weekend. Do you two want a snack? I think we still have some orange sherbet."

Brandon went off into a gale of uncontrollable laughter.

"I'd love some *sherbet*," Bethany said. "I think it's a perfect day for *sherbet*."

"I want orange . . . *sherbet!*" Brandon managed to get the word out before another tidal wave of hysterics engulfed him.

"Three orange *sherbets*, coming right up," Bethany's mother said.

"Maybe I'll write a new poem," Bethany said. " 'Ode to *Sherbet* in Springtime.' "

Bethany took her bowl of sherbet upstairs. She was going to spend the rest of the afternoon crossing off problems on her problems list. Maybe she would even tear the problems list into little teensy, tiny pieces and throw them all away, or bury them in Jane's yard, beneath her tree fort. But first she sat on her window seat for a long, long time, looking out at the mountains, savoring the sweetness of the sherbet, thinking about nothing, and smiling.